The BEAST and the BETHANY

Battle of the Beast

*For my beloved sister Kitty, and her beastly bear Rufus. You can
battle it out to see who's more deserving of this dedication.*
J. M. P.

For Nani and Fefe.
I. F.

First published in Great Britain 2022 by Farshore

An imprint of HarperCollins*Publishers*
1 London Bridge Street
London SE1 9GF

HarperCollins*Publishers*
1st Floor, Watemarque Building, Ringsend Road
Dublin 4, Ireland

Text Copyright © 2022 Jack Meggitt-Phillips
Illustrations copyright © 2022 Isabelle Follath

The moral rights of the author and cover illustrator have been asserted

ISBN 978 1 4052 9893 3

farshore.co.uk

A CIP catalogue record for this title is available from the British Library

Printed and bound in the UK using 100% renewable electricity at CPI Group (UK) Ltd
1

The BEAST and the BETHANY

Battle of the Beast

Jack Meggitt-Phillips
Illustrated by Isabelle Follath

The Feathery Feast

The only thing left of Wintloria was the forest, and there wasn't much of that left any more.

The trees were said to possess an ancient and beguiling form of magic – leaves that could wipe away scars, fruit nourishing enough to sustain an entire family for a week, bark that could scratch any itch, no matter how irksome or inconveniently located. As a result, the forest attracted much unwanted attention from the sort of people who couldn't appreciate beauty unless they could chop it down and make it their own.

As the forest grew smaller and the trophy hunters grew greedier, many of the animals deserted its branches.

However, there was one group of creatures who stubbornly refused to leave.

There were only nineteen Wintlorian purple-breasted parrots left in the world, and nearly all of them lived in the Wintorian rainforest. They were a noisy and deeply impractical species, constantly searching for opportunities to sing another song or host another feathery fashion show, when they should have been worrying about their own existence.

On this particular day, the parrots had gathered in the hollow trunk of the largest tree to celebrate their third feast of the week. The first feast had been thrown to mark the queen's favourite corgi's half-birthday, while the second had been to celebrate the fact that one of the parrots had finally found the piece of string she had been looking for all afternoon. This third feast, however, promised to be a very special one indeed.

Every parrot was dressed in their featheriest finery. They were all laying delicious egg-shaped meals for each other, and the volume of their songs was already approaching a level that some may have termed 'rowdy'. At the top of the tree, a young male parrot named Mortimer was hanging up a banner that read: WELCOME HOME, CLAUDETTE.

"Spiffy-whiff sign, Morty!" said Giulietta, an extremely well-dressed older parrot. "Need a spot of help hanging the thing up?"

Mortimer grimaced. For one thing, the only person he allowed to call him 'Morty' was Claudette. For another, he hated his species' obsession with always having to do things *together*.

"I'm fine," he snapped. "I don't need anyone's help."

"I know you don't *need* the help," said Giulietta, "but it's nice to have it all the same, what-what? If we only focused on the things we needed in life, then there would no such thing as the cha-cha – ooh, or the blueberry cheesecake."

Thrilled with her own marvellous observation, Giulietta started humming the tune to a cha-cha, as she wiggled her sizeable bottom and laid an egg containing a blueberry cheesecake. She flew up and grabbed one end of Mortimer's banner.

"Get off!" shouted Mortimer, as he tugged it away from her.

"I shall do no such thing," said Giulietta, tugging right back. "Every parrot knows that four talons are better than two."

The tug of war continued – Giulietta determined to

offer help, Mortimer even more determined not to accept it – until the banner ripped down the middle.

"Whoopsie-poopsie," said Giulietta.

"Whoopsie-poopsie?!" spluttered Mortimer. "I spent all week working on this so it would be perfect for Claudette, and now you've ruined it, you blithering twerp!"

Giulietta's eyes filled with purple tears. She wasn't used to hearing such unfriendly words in the forest because all Wintlorians were supposed to be kind to each other and the world around them.

"S-s-sorry, M-M-Morty," she stammered. "I should have been more c-c-careful."

"You should never have bothered me in the first place," said Mortimer. "Go away and make someone else's life a misery instead."

Giulietta flapped her way back down to the bottom of the tree, raining purple tears. Mortimer hung up the larger part of the banner, which now read: ME HOME, CLAUDETTE.

He was irritated to find that he was feeling guilty about how he had treated Giulietta, even though she was the one who had destroyed the banner. He knew that Claudette would make him apologise when she got there, so, reluctantly, he swooped down to the bottom of the tree.

The hollow trunk was a chaos of purple, with every bird singing and dancing a merry tune about the return of their favourite parrot. They sang about the exquisite fluffiness of Claudette's feathers, the honey-dipped silkiness of her voice, and the kindness she showed to everyone she met. There was even an entire verse dedicated to the sparkle in her left eye.

Unlike the rest of his species, Mortimer was not a fan of feasts. Usually, he made excuses to avoid them, and had only made an exception for this one because of his affection for Claudette. In fact, out of all the parrots in the forest, Mortimer was probably the one who loved Claudette the most. She had acted as a mother to him after his parents had been killed by trophy hunters.

If Mortimer had been a singing or dancing sort of parrot, then he could have led a verse that would have moved the rest of the tree to tears. He wondered whether he should give it a go, for Claudette's sake. Reluctantly, and shaking ever so slightly, he stepped further into the gathering. But, before he could sing a note, or give his bottom so much as a wiggle, the whole forest began to shake.

A puddle grew out of the ground in front of the tree. At

first it looked like any normal puddle – the sort you might find on a pavement after a rainy day, or in a gym after an especially sweaty game of dodgeball. But then it started to spit and hiss.

"She's on her way!" said Mortimer in excitement. "Any moment now, Claudette will be here!"

For the past few weeks, Claudette had been in the care of the **D**ivision **of R**emoving **R**apscallions **i**n**S**ecret (D.o.R.R.i.S. among friends), a secret organisation whose agents travelled almost exclusively via puddle portals. None of the parrots were entirely sure why Claudette needed to be looked after by D.o.R.R.i.S. in the first place, but they were all terribly excited to see her. Mortimer fluffed his feathers to make sure they were at their very best, while the others sang Claudette's song at an increasingly hysterical volume.

The puddle spat out three D.o.R.R.i.S. agents, otherwise known as Dorrises: one human, another humanish and the final one not human at all. They were all sporting weapons as varied as their appearances.

"Who's the highest-ranking parrot here? I have a special message from D.o.R.R.i.S. head agent, Mr Nicholas Nickle," said Agent Hughie, a suave human being with a laser gun.

"There is no ranking system in Wintloria," answered one of the parrots in a sing-song voice. "Every man, parrot and toad lives equally in this forest."

"That is simply not acceptable," said Agent Louie, a humanish agent with orange scales instead of skin. "There must be someone in charge. We can't conduct a conversation with all of you at once."

"Why ever not? We Wintlorians are all charming conversationalists. Try us on any topic, and I promise we won't disappoint," answered a different parrot.

"Name . . . a . . . leader," hissed Agent Stewie, who looked like the result of what might happen if a cactus fell in love with a large possum. "If you don't, we won't be able to portal Claudette to this location."

"I'm in charge," said Mortimer, stepping forward. "Give us Claudette, now."

There was murmuring aplenty from the other parrots. None would say it aloud, but all were thinking that if there was a leader of their species, it certainly wouldn't be Mortimer.

Agent Hughie bent over, nose to beak with the young parrot. "What is your name, rank and occupation?"

"None of your business, none of your business and none of your business," answered Mortimer. "Where's Claudette?"

Agent Hughie clicked at Agent Louie, who presented Mortimer with an incomprehensible medical chart. Agent Stewie hissed coordinates into a peculiar radio.

"Mr Nickle felt we should warn you about Claudette's condition, because we know she's been hiding the truth," said Agent Hughie. "She didn't want to worry you all."

"What are you talking about?" asked Mortimer. His tone was sharp and unfriendly, but inside he was jittery with fear and worry. "Just tell me."

"Claudette has been in contact with a creature as dark, dangerous and prickly as a hedgehog waiting in the shadows with a torpedo," said Agent Louie. "We've done what we can for her, but there's something blocking her recovery. Her experience with . . . this thing . . . has left her weak."

"She's lucky to be alive at all," hissed Agent Stewie with a shudder. "Wherever this creature goes, death and destruction usually follow."

"What creature?" asked Mortimer. "Why aren't any of you speaking its name?"

The three agents shared a glance.

"We just wanted you to be prepared," said Agent Hughie, as he nodded to Agent Stewie. "Mr Nickle felt it was the least you deserved."

Agent Stewie fiddled with a high-tech device that looked awfully like an umbrella. The puddle portal started to hiss and spit again – more angrily this time.

The parrots at the back, who hadn't heard the conversation, started whooping, cheering and singing the song of Claudette again. The other parrots joined in, hoping to steel their nerves with the song, but Mortimer kept his beak closed.

The singing grew louder and the puddle grew hissier and more spitful, until something purple burst out. The singing immediately stopped.

The something purple was Claudette.

It took a moment for the parrots to recognise her, because she had changed so very much. Her once splendid feathers were now pale and patchy, the sparkle in both her eyes had dimmed, and she was using a small crutch under one of her wings. She tried her hardest to put a smile across her beak.

"Hullo, poppets," she said. Her beautiful voice was raspy and cracked. "It's so very nice to see you all. Shall we sing a –?"

Claudette was trying to be brave but the exertion was too much for her. She wobbled on her talons and fell to the floor.

Mortimer immediately flew to her side. The other parrots fetched leaves, barks, fruit and other secrets of the forest that might heal her ailments. Mortimer cradled Claudette in his small wings, demonstrating a delicacy and a gentleness that none of the other parrots had seen before.

"Claudette . . . I . . ." began Mortimer.

He didn't know what to say. Last time he had seen Claudette, she had been able to get through an entire concert without breaking a sweat. Now she couldn't even get through a sentence. The sight of his favourite parrot in the world looking so weak made him feel terrified and powerless – but, above all, absolutely furious.

"Who did this to you, Claudette?" Mortimer tried using his softest voice, but it just came out bitter and hard. "Give me a name!"

"The beast," murmured Claudette. Using the little strength she had left, she sat up and whispered urgently into his ear, "I've seen into the beast's mind, Morty: its dreadful deeds, its awful memories. And yet nothing compares to the things that it wants to do to a girl named Bethany. Save her, Morty. Do whatever it takes, and SAVE BETHANY."

The No-Beast and the Bethany

"LET ME GOOO!" Bethany cried, as the beast's two fat tongues slithered around her neck like a pair of greedy cobras.

She was trapped in the glowing red walls of a D.o.R.R.i.S. laser cage. Her best friend, the young 512-year-old Ebenezer Tweezer, was lying dead on the floor.

"Oh, I don't think so," said the beast. Bethany had no idea how it was still able to speak, because she couldn't see its face. "This particular feast has been a long time coming, and I have every intention of enjoying my supper."

As the beast spoke, more and more tongues wrapped

themselves around Bethany – first slithering around her sneakers and jeans, then covering her jumper, before two more headed straight for her face.

"Did you really think you could escape me?" asked the beast. Bethany wriggled and writhed, as she felt herself being dragged towards the beast's dribbling, stinking mouth. "Didn't you realise the truth? I always have another scheme up my sleeves."

The beast let out a deep, slithery chuckle. As Bethany was dragged closer to her death, she realised that this was inevitable. She'd never had a chance of defeating the beast.

And then, just as she was about to be chomped to pieces, Bethany woke up.

She found herself tossing and turning in her bedroom

of the fifteen-storey house. She was soaking wet. At first, she thought she was drenched in the beast's dribble, before she realised that it was just her own sweat. She patted her body, furiously checking that every limb, finger, knuckle and kneecap was still there, unchomped and ready to use.

She jumped unsteadily out of bed. Her legs were still trembling, and she had to rub her eyes a few times to make absolutely certain that she wasn't actually trapped in the beast's cage.

"Stupid, stupid brain," she grumbled. "Why do you always have to give me nightmares?"

Her brain had been tormenting her with nightmares for months – ever since she had last seen the beast in its cage. Sometimes her mind had devised elaborate scenarios involving exploding teapots and volcanic beehives; other times it had kept things classic with a simple head-chomping.

It always took Bethany a few moments to recover. She was forever grateful that the creature who had almost eaten her alive (twice) was trapped in some faraway cage. If her legs hadn't still been trembling, she might even have attempted to jump for joy.

Bethany got dressed and stomped out of the room, determined to put the whole thing behind her. She hadn't told anyone about her nightmares, because speaking about them somehow made them more real.

When she got downstairs, she found Ebenezer worriedly looking out of the window. Usually, Bethany liked to begin her day by pranking Ebenezer, or making fun of his stupid waistcoats, but there was something about seeing him dead in her dreams that put her in a more generous mood. She ran over and treated him to an ever so slightly terrifying grin.

"Morning, gitface!" She took a moment to compose herself, because she was never very good at saying soppy things. "I just want you to know . . . I'm really glad you haven't been horribly murdered."

Ebenezer turned away from the window and blinked at her a few times. This was one of the nicest things that

Bethany had ever said to him, and he had no idea what he had done to deserve it.

"Thank you, Bethany," said Ebenezer. He wasn't too good at the soppy stuff either, so he took a deep breath. "I . . . well, I'm delighted that you haven't been horribly murdered either."

Bethany flashed her terrifying grin again, before stomping through to the kitchen. She picked up a hammer and started bashing a poor, defenceless muffin to death, while Ebenezer returned his attention to the window.

"Anyone there yet?" shouted Bethany.

Outside on the lawn, Ebenezer had put up a rather heroic-looking portrait of himself, standing upon a mountaintop. Next to this, there was a sign that read:

DO-GOODING OPEN HOUSE

Got a problem? Ring the bell, and Mr Tweezer will solve it. Please form an orderly queue.

Unfortunately, there was no queue to be formed – orderly or otherwise. There wasn't even so much as a pigeon upon the lawn.

"It doesn't make any sense," said Ebenezer. "It's like

the neighbourhood doesn't want any of my gorgeous help."

As part of their do-gooding mission, Ebenezer had set up The Wise Tweezer – a problem-solving business that consulted on any issue, no matter how big or small. At the beginning, he had entertained dozens of clients but, one by one, they had all fallen away. In an attempt to get them back, and promote the business, he had commissioned an artist to paint him in a variety of provocative poses and outfits.

"Maybe I should put out the portrait of me saving Lord Tibbles from a tree instead," said Ebenezer. "My eyes really sparkle in that one."

"Or maybe you should just accept that people aren't gonna come visiting today," said Bethany. "Maybe they've had enough of your unique kind of . . . help."

"Poppycock! The Wise Tweezer is nothing short of a triumph. After five centuries of living, it's no wonder that I'm so very wisdomous," said Ebenezer. "Why, only yesterday the bird-keeper asked if I could help his hoatzin smell less like an egg sandwich that's been left out in the sun for a few decades. I took a long, hard sit-down in the Contemplation Chambers on the fourth floor. I dedicated so much time to the problem that I missed lunch and afternoon tea."

"Yeah, but what did you actually do about it?" asked Bethany.

"Well, after oodles of noodle-scratching, I realised that I couldn't help the poor fellow. I explained to the bird-keeper that I am not, nor have I ever been, a hoatzin – and therefore couldn't possibly be expected to understand the smells of one," said Ebenezer. "I sent him away with a pat on the back and a promise that I would do my utmost to help him with any other problems he might have in the future. He didn't show it, but I could tell that he was terribly moved by all the effort that I had put into his little problem."

Bethany smirked. Nearly all of Ebenezer's do-gooding projects ended with him telling neighbours that he couldn't help them after all. She was going to point out that spending his days sitting in the Contemplation Chambers wasn't all that helpful but, for once, she bit her tongue. It had taken a long time to get Ebenezer interested in do-gooding, and she didn't want to say anything that might dampen his enthusiasm.

"You're right – we're both doing a *lot* of good," said Bethany, in her least sarcastic voice. She scattered her muffin corpse between two slices of bread and picked up a bottle of squirty mayonnaise from the fridge. "And we're able to do it, 'cause no one's getting in our way. It's like our friend Claudette says – once you remove the bad from your life, the good finds it a lot easier to move in."

"She's a wise parrot," said Ebenezer. He was always slightly uncomfortable whenever Claudette was mentioned, because he felt guilty about everything that the beast had done to her. "How is she?"

"She's supposed to be back in Wintloria today," said Bethany. "She's gonna send us her address so we can write LOADS of postcards to each other."

"Oh, how marvellous! I can't wait to tell her all about the wonders of The Wise Tweezer," said Ebenezer, clapping his hands. "She's going to be so proud of how far we've moved on from the beast."

Bethany shuddered at the mention of the beast. She squeezed the squirty bottle like a stress ball, and accidentally caused a mayonnaise explosion. Fortunately, explosions were pretty commonplace around Bethany's sandwiches, so Ebenezer didn't pay much attention.

"Speaking of which, how's it all going at Miss Muddle's sweet shop?" asked Ebenezer.

"Yeah, fine, I guess," said Bethany. She scrunched her eyes shut and tried to push all thoughts of the beast out of her mind.

"You don't sound very enthusiastic," said Ebenezer. He sauntered over to give Bethany a patronising pat on the shoulder. "I know it must be a little intimidating sharing a house with a do-gooder as splendid as myself, but there's no need to feel insecure. I'm sure you'll catch up with me at some point. And if you need any help, The Wise Tweezer is always on the lookout for new employees."

Bethany scowled at Ebenezer. It took every ounce of her restraint not to squirt the mayonnaise bottle at him, and tell him exactly what everyone really thought of his business.

"As a matter of fact, it's actually going pretty flipping awesomely," said Bethany. She demayonnaised herself, and ate the salvageable parts of her breakfast sandwich. "Miss Muddle said she's been totally impressed with how I've helped her deliver the happiness hampers to people in the neighbourhood. She says she wants to give me a reward. She didn't say what it was, but she says it's gonna prove to everyone, once and for all, that I am a do-gooder!"

Ebenezer's face fell. He knew he should be happy for Bethany, but he didn't much like the idea that people might think she was a better do-gooder than him.

"Aren't you gonna say well done?" asked Bethany. "If you don't, I'm gonna decapitate all your bath toys, and put superglue on all your –"

Bethany was interrupted by the phone brring-brringing from the hallway.

"Maybe it's someone who wants my help," said Ebenezer with excitement. "You answer it, Bethany. Make it sound as though I am extremely busy and important. And, whatever you do, do *not* make me sound desperate."

Bethany scowled as she picked up the phone. "Oi-oi, what do you flipping want then?"

"*Bethany!*" said Ebenezer. "Remember our fancy phone voice training!"

Bethany rolled her eyes, and put on a slightly less aggressive voice. "Sozza. I mean, *hello*. This is the house of Bethany and Tweezer, what do you flipping want?"

There was a crackle on the other end of the line. A few seconds later, Bethany heard the rasping, jangly voice of D.o.R.R.i.S. head agent, Mr Nicholas Nickle.

"*Squeezer, Bethany, is that you?*" asked Mr Nickle. The line was patchy because the old man was several thousands of miles away. "*We have . . . serious . . . with the beast, and I ne– your help.*

The Panic and the Muddle

"*The beast . . . unlike anything I've ever seen,*" said Mr Nickle. "*We need some– who can . . . the beast.*" Ebenezer wondered why Bethany's hand was gripped so tightly around the phone. She turned round – and, with a single look, he knew who the call was from.

"Nickle says there's something going on with the beast," she said.

"Has he opened up a puddle portal for us? I'll get the D.o.R.R.i.S. wellies," said Ebenezer.

"I've got a better idea," said Bethany.

She slammed down the phone. Ebenezer's mouth dropped open.

"You can't hang up on D.o.R.R.i.S.!" he said.

"Can and did," said Bethany, trying to sound confident. "It's for our own good."

"But, but, but . . . shouldn't we try and –" began Ebenezer.

"WE ARE NEVER SEEING THAT DRIBBLY STINKER AGAIN!" shouted Bethany.

"I, er . . . oh, fine then," said Ebenezer, even though he was feeling in a distinctly un-oh-fine-then mood. Caged or not, it felt like a mistake to ignore the beast – especially when there were secret agencies involved. "If it's important to you, I'll make it important to me. I read a comic about friendship a few decades ago, and it said that this sort of thing is very important."

The phone started brring-brringing again. Bethany and Ebenezer gave it much the same stare as someone who has returned home to find a wild bear in their living room. Bethany unplugged the phone from the wall.

"Do NOT plug it back in," she said.

"We can't just act as if nothing's happened!" said Ebenezer.

"Yeah we can," said Bethany. She pulled her backpack over her shoulders and headed for the door. "Come on – you're driving me to the sweet shop."

Bethany dragged Ebenezer into the car for the shortish

drive to Miss Muddle's sweet shop.

"Look here, are you absolutely positive that we shouldn't –?" began Ebenezer.

"That conversation with Nickle didn't happen, and this conversation isn't happening either," said Bethany. "Stop driving like a granny, and get moving."

Ebenezer slowed his pace because he didn't care to be bossed about in his own car. However, he soon came to regret it.

He had distributed many of his specially commissioned paintings around the neighbourhood, complete with information about services that The Wise Tweezer could offer. Ebenezer usually drove past too fast to pay them much attention, but now that he was going slowly, he saw that unfavourable changes had been made.

The paintings had been graffitied with unibrows, stupid hairdos and twirly-whirly moustaches. Many of them had been given unfavourable speech bubbles. For instance, the painting of Ebenezer dressed in his best tennis clothes, which had been hanging so wonderfully outside the library, now had a speech bubble reading 'I am a twerp', while the more formally dressed Ebenezer outside the Cussock Theatre simply read 'USELESS'.

As they passed the louche loungewear painting outside the zoo, Ebenezer spotted some handwriting he recognised.

"Did . . . did *you* do that one, Bethany?" he asked. "My waistcoats do *not* make me look stupid."

"Sozza, I was bored on my way home one day. And besides, my message actually covered up one that was way more mean," said Bethany. She saw Ebenezer's face fall. "Whoops. Probably shouldn't have said that."

Ebenezer was crushed. "Haven't people enjoyed the work of The Wise Tweezer? Why didn't you tell me before?"

"Didn't wanna upset you," said Bethany. "Don't worry,

though. If I find the people who are leaving the really mean messages, I'll replace their cushions with cactuses."

Ebenezer pulled up outside the sweet shop feeling terribly glum, while Bethany was desperately trying to steer her thoughts away from the beast. She always loved helping Miss Muddle with the hampers, so she tried her very best to focus on this instead. Also, today was particularly exciting, because she was going to find out how Miss Muddle was going to reward her for all the hard work.

Bethany jumped out of the car and barged through the doors, with Ebenezer plodding slowly behind. The sweet shop was empty, and Miss Muddle was at the till – elbows deep in her new sweet creation, the bombastic bubbletrumpet.

"Hello, sweeties!" said Miss Muddle. It took a moment for Bethany and Ebenezer to realise she was speaking to them, because she was often in the habit of talking to her own creations. "How are my two favourite lollipop lickers?"

Ebenezer was going to answer that he really wasn't feeling too cheery at all, and that if there were any lollipops going, then he could really do with one.

"We're both flipping awesome," said Bethany. "How's the new sweet going?"

Miss Muddle pulled her arms out of the bombastic bubbletrumpet, causing it to tootle a mournful tune. She frowned, as though it were a rude party guest, and ran a hand through her wild mop of blue hair.

"We must always remain hopeful, no matter how much the sweets try to make us look like fools," she said. "Ready to get hampering?"

Bethany grabbed her apron – somehow, even messier than Miss Muddle's – and took out the ingredients for the latest sandwich filling that they'd been working on: a tub of marmite, a jug of pineapple juice and a few squirts of goats' cheese.

She also removed the crumpled photograph of the moustachioed man, the moustacheless woman and the scowling baby version of herself from her back pocket, because she liked the idea that her parents might be watching her putting the sandwiches together.

As Bethany sandwiched, Miss Muddle started whipping up swirly fondants. Ebenezer was left feeling useless again, so he perched himself on one of the cleaner worktops.

He watched Bethany merrily stomp around her worktop, and felt incredibly jealous. It was a huge blow to realise that he was completely failing on the do-gooding front, and the call from Mr Nickle had felt like confirmation of the fact that Ebenezer would never really be able to escape from the bad he had done in his past.

Miss Muddle came over to inspect the state of Bethany's sandwich platter. She raised her blue brows at the banana skins that Bethany had added as a last-minute whim.

"Now then, what did we say about these?" she asked.

"That they were a totally awesome idea?" said Bethany.

"We said that experimental is good, but *edible* is better," said Miss Muddle. She removed some sandwich tweezers from her lab coat, and plucked out the skins. "Ready to try one, Mr Tweezer?"

Ebenezer was readier to sit on one of Bethany's cactus cushions.

"This one's gonna be awesome," said Bethany.

This didn't inspire Ebenezer with confidence. Bethany was regularly delighted with her recipes, regardless of whether they were exquisite or excruciating. However, there was no way of getting out of eating a sandwich without hurting her feelings.

"I can't wait," he said unconvincingly, as he picked one up.

"Hurry up. The pineapple juice is gonna leak out if you

leave it much longer," she said.

Ebenezer scrunched his eyes shut and took the nibbliest nibble possible. He was surprised to find that the nibble was nothing short of nomalicious.

"Bethany, this is remarkable!" he said.

Bethany scowled. "Why are you so surprised?"

"I'm not surprised," he said, a little too quickly. "It's just that . . . well, you're right. This is your best one yet. It makes all the others look like microwaved pigeon vomit."

"It's not *that* good," said Bethany, crossing her arms. "I've made plenty of other awesome ones. Remember that cod and custard one I made? *Without* Miss Muddle's help."

Ebenezer remembered it well. It had made him consider snipping off his tongue with the kitchen scissors.

"Well, you should just make this recipe from now on," said Ebenezer. Then he added sadly, "I can't believe you're even good at making sandwiches now."

"In fairness, she does have an *extremely* good teacher," said Miss Muddle. "I've loaded up the drinks fountain in the corner. Shall we give them smoothies in today's hamper, or perhaps something of a more chocolatey variety?"

They decided to put a collection of each into the hampers. Ebenezer glumly filled up some empty glass bottles at the fountain, while Miss Muddle used the opportunity to grill Bethany on her sweet-making knowledge.

"Please tell me the exact length of time that a baby tarantula can hold their breath, and then would you be good enough to tell us the size of Planck's constant?"

Bethany collected the rest of the hamper things, while Miss Muddle bombarded her with questions on topics including French poetry, exotic weeds and the results of the 1946 Ladies' Volleyball Championships. Miss Muddle was a firm believer that a sweet-maker could never know too much about the world, and she was constantly giving Bethany books, records, videos, photographs and random scribbles on pieces of paper in an attempt to improve her mind.

"Right – I'm done," said Bethany. She went to grab the hamper destined for the children's hospital, but Miss Muddle got there first and held it over her head.

"Not so fast, young lady. I'm still waiting to hear the size of Planck's constant," she said.

"Fine. Planck's constant is tiny. Tinier than even the crumbliest crumb of a cupcake. That's what it said in that stupid *Quantum Mechanics for Morons* book you gave me anyway," said Bethany. "Hey, Muddle, I've got a question for you. Where's this flipping reward you were talking about?"

"Bumbling bonbons, I almost forgot!" said Miss Muddle. She ran into the Concoction Room, and returned with a shiny gold piece of card. "I've decided to throw you a party!"

"You've decided to throw her a what?!" asked Ebenezer.

Miss Muddle was an absent-minded, scruffy writer, but Ebenezer could just about make out her scrawl.

GOSH ISN'T BETHANY BRILLIANT?
JOIN US ON FRIDAY FOR A CELEBRATION OF
ALL THINGS BETHANY. ONE OF THE KINDEST,
MOST HARD-WORKING PEOPLE IN THIS
NEIGHBOURHOOD. SWEETS WILL BE PROVIDED,
BUT PLEASE BRING YOUR OWN COMPLIMENTS.

Bethany scowled as she read it. "Is this a prank?"

"Absolutely not. I left my pranking days behind me long ago. These days, all my mischief goes into my shop," said Miss Muddle. "And I remember, when I stopped being bad, how much I wanted people to notice how I'd changed. I know you like to pretend that you don't care what people think –"

"I *don't* care what people think," said Bethany.

"Of course you don't. And you can show people just how much you don't care, on Friday," said Miss Muddle. "I sent the invitations around the neighbourhood this morning. It's a surprise party – SURPRISE!"

Bethany didn't know how to react, because this was the kindest thing that anyone had ever done for her.

"I don't think you're supposed to shout surprise until the day of the party," said Ebenezer. He also didn't know how to react, because he was literally turning a little bit green with envy. "You know, so the person who's getting the party is actually surprised?"

"Is that right? Sorry. I don't think I've actually been to a surprise party. Or many parties at all, actually," said Miss Muddle. She handed Bethany the children's hospital hamper and looked up at the candy-cane clock. "Time for you two to get going. We've got plenty of time to talk parties, and balloons and . . . ooh, hold on a mo, what's that horrid, shrill sound? I keep hearing it."

"I believe it's the telephone, Miss Muddle," said Ebenezer, glad at last to be useful.

"Oh, that would make a lot of sense," said Miss Muddle. She rummaged through the pick 'n' mix trolley until she found her candy-cane shaped phone. "Oh hell?" she said.

"Sorry, I mean – hello?"

Miss Muddle listened for a few moments. She turned to Ebenezer and Bethany.

"It's a call for you two," she said, frowning at the receiver. "It's an old man, but I think he said his name was Dorris. He says he's tracked the nearest phone to your location, and that he needs to speak to you right away, about a beat, or maybe some sort of feast?"

Ebenezer decided to be more like Bethany and DO something. He snatched the phone from Miss Muddle.

"Listen carefully now, Mr Nickle," said Ebenezer. He cleared his throat, and used his very fanciest phone voice, so that his message would be understood. "BOG. OFF."

Ebenezer slammed down the receiver. He informed Miss Muddle to ignore any and all future calls she may receive from that number, grabbed a hamper, and left the shop with Bethany.

The Close Calls

Unfortunately, Mr Nickle was not the sort of man who accepted directions of a bogging nature. Everywhere Ebenezer and Bethany went, they were haunted by his calls.

He called all the departments in the hospital, while Bethany and Ebenezer were delivering hampers to the children's ward. He called every telephone box in the area as they handed out hampers at the homeless shelter.

Next up was the retirement home. Bethany didn't much care for the place, but Ebenezer adored comparing their wrinkled, wizened faces with his own wonderfully creaseless one. As they walked into the home's lounge and opened up the hampers, the wrinkly faces in the room crinkled with joy at the various sweets, sandwiches and smoothies on offer.

"Excuse me," said one of the wrinkly minxes – a former showgirl, who could still do the splits at the age of eighty-nine. "Would it be possible to take a photograph?"

Ebenezer smiled smugly, as the showgirl handed him the old-fashioned camera. He was excellent at photographs, because he had spent a lot of time sitting for portraits in the Posing Gallery of the fifteen-storey house.

"Which would you prefer from me, dear lady? A playful pout, or an ear-to-ear grin?" he asked, as he cosied up next to her.

"I think you've misunderstood me," said the showgirl. "I don't want to have a photograph with you. I want you to take one of me and your friend."

"You want one with *Bethany*?" said Ebenezer. "But I'm much prettier!"

"Just take the photograph," said the showgirl. She pushed Ebenezer away and put her arms around a perplexed Bethany. "Say cheese!"

"Say it yourself, you lazy git," said Bethany. The scowl on her face deepened as the showgirl grinned and did the splits next to her.

"Can I have one taken with you as well?" asked another

oldie in a moth-eaten jumper.

"Why?" asked Bethany suspiciously.

"Why? I want proof of meeting one of the kindest people in the world!" said the oldie.

Bethany had never been called kind before. She walked over to the oldie, and scowled even harder as Ebenezer grumpily snapped the camera.

Soon everyone wanted a picture with Bethany – and all of them showered her with compliments that she didn't know how to accept. She responded by pulling rude faces in all the pictures.

As Ebenezer irritably snapped the final snap, Nurse Mindy came over.

"I read Miss Muddle's invitation out to them earlier, and they were all so excited to see you again, Bethany," she said. She looked pointedly at Ebenezer. "It's so nice to have someone in the neighbourhood who's doing *actual* good."

"What are you talking about? The Wise Tweezer offered you some *excellent* problem-solving, Nurse Mindy!" said Ebenezer.

Nurse Mindy snorted. "I asked you to help us with the home's hearing-aid system. But after three weeks in your 'Contemplation Chambers', the only idea you came up with was for us all to speak using megaphones!"

"I thought it was a good idea," said Ebenezer quietly.

"Hey, don't be mean to him," said Bethany, targeting her scowl at Nurse Mindy. "He's trying his best."

"It would be best for everyone if he didn't try at all," said Nurse Mindy. "By the way, there's a call for both of you at reception. We said you were busy, but apparently you're the only ones who can help with some sort of feet, or yeast problem he's having."

"Tell him we're not here," said Bethany.

Then, to turn their lie into a truth, Ebenezer and Bethany

left the retirement home. As they climbed back into the car, Bethany frowned.

"Dunno why Mr Nickle's even bothering," she said. "There's nothing he can say that'll make us see the beast again. We're a team on this."

Ebenezer was still fuming about the fact that no one wanted to take a picture of him, or throw him a lovely party, or even take his excellent advice on megaphones. If he and Bethany were a team, then he was definitely the weakest player.

"Did you hear me, gitface?" said Bethany, thwacking him. "I said we're a team."

"Oh yes," said Ebenezer, absent-mindedly. "Perhaps we should purchase some matching outfits."

"Nah, you're all right – I wouldn't be seen dead in the stupid things you wear," said Bethany. She removed the golden invitation from her backpack. "But, as my number one teammate, I've decided that you're gonna play an important role in my party. Dunno what the role will be yet, but it'll be a doozy."

"How kind of you," said Ebenezer stiffly. The last thing he wanted to do was talk more about the party.

"Maybe I'll invite Claudette as well. She told me that

Wintlorian purple-breasted parrots *love* parties," said Bethany. "Although, actually, I don't think she's up to flying yet, so we'll just have to take lots of photos for her. Ooh! Maybe that could be your role at the party. You were a great photographer back in the retirement home."

Ebenezer grimaced. A party spent as Bethany's official photographer sounded like torture.

They made it to their final stop of the day – the orphanage. Ebenezer pulled in to the creaky, crumbling gates. He had heard that most homes for children were kind places, overflowing with love and nourishment, but this place had always looked like it wanted to stomp on sandcastles and spit phlegm into people's tea.

As Ebenezer was being struck by the ugliness of the place, he almost struck a child with the car. The child was a kind-faced, jumper-wearing chap, who treated the near-death experience with remarkable good grace.

"Oh, ah, so sorry, Mr Tweezer. I didn't mean to get in the way, I just got so excited when I saw your car from the window," said Geoffrey. "Everyone else is inside playing with rocks."

"Don't be an idiot, Geoffrey. I should be the one saying sorry," said Ebenezer, crossly. "I suppose I shouldn't really be calling you an idiot after nearly killing you either."

"Oh, ah, don't worry. It's awfully nice of you to say anything to me at all," said Geoffrey. He poked his head into Ebenezer's side of the car and beamed at Bethany. "HULLO THERE!" he said, before realising he had spoken with far too much enthusiasm, "Oh, ah, I mean 'hullo' – yes, yes that's at a far more normal sort of volume. How . . . um, well, if it's not too much of a personal question . . . how are you?"

"Pretty awesome, actually," said Bethany. She jumped out of the car with the last of the hampers. "Not sure if you've heard, but it's basically been confirmed that I'm the number one do-gooder in this neighbourhood. Miss Muddle's holding a party to prove it on Friday."

"Oh wowzers, that's brilliant!" said Geoffrey. Nervously, he added, "I hope you won't forget me now you're famous."

"Don't worry, Geoffers, I'll never forget you," said Bethany. "As a matter of fact, 'cause you're so important to me, I'm gonna make sure you have a very special party role."

Ebenezer grimaced again. He wanted to be the only one with a role at Bethany's party, even if it was just taking stupid photographs

"Oh, how kind of you! And, actually, I've got something

that might help you celebrate," beamed Geoffrey. He removed a brightly illustrated thing from the back of his trousers. "It's the latest issue of *D.I. Tortoise: Fast Thinker, Slow Walker!*"

Bethany thumbed the comic thoughtfully, like a cheese connoisseur inspecting a new kind of Brie. "Has this one got any more Professor Moleyarty in it?" she asked.

"Not until right at the end. The main villain is one of his agents, the Reichenbach Fowl," said Geoffrey. He tried and failed to say the next bit as casually as possible. "Apparently there's a *D.I. Tortoise* movie coming out soon. I thought that maybe we could –?"

"In some ways, I'm a bit of a D.I. Tortoise myself," said Bethany, her attention absorbed by the comic. "Helping the world, defeating evil. I'm basically kind of a superhero."

Ebenezer laughed. Bethany scowled at him.

"That reminds me, I've brought something for you, Geoffers," said Bethany. She reached into her backpack and produced one of Miss Muddle's whistlepip wonders. "It's nothing special."

"Whistlepip wonders are my absolute favourite!" said Geoffrey.

"I know," said Bethany, blushing slightly.

Geoffrey disappeared the wonder with a single, satisfied

gulp. "Mmm," he said. "Oh, it's so nice to have something to eat again. Timothy forgot to feed us last night . . . and this morning."

"He did WHAT?" asked Bethany.

"Oh, ah, it's no big deal," said Geoffrey quickly. "He was probably too busy with his paperwork. I don't want to get anyone into trouble."

"Too late," said Bethany. "We're putting a stop to this – NOW. D.I. Bethany is on the case!"

She stomped into the orphanage and up the creaky stairs which led to the director's office, with Geoffrey struggling to keep up with her. Ebenezer followed more slowly, still feeling grumpy about – well, everything.

Timothy Skittle, the director of the orphanage, was pacing up and down the room. He had bitten all of his fingernails to stubs, and his desk was groaning with even more paper than usual.

"Every time I finish one file, another ten arrive!" he moaned to himself.

The splintery floor creaked under Bethany's feet. Timothy flicked his head around and inspected the three of them with fear in his eyes. He looked enviously at their fingernails, as if he was considering giving them a chew.

"Why do I have to deal with so many *children*?" said Timothy, speaking the word as if it were a deadly fungus. "If you've come here for your file, then I'm sorry, but I don't know where I've put it."

"File?" asked Ebenezer.

"The file all children are meant to be given when they leave the orphanage. My predecessor Miss Fizzlewick never did any of it, because she said paperwork was far too *unladylike*," said Timothy. He moaned with self-pity. "She's left me with so much work to do! I just can't stand it!"

"You know what I can't stand?" said Bethany. "People who don't remember to feed my friends."

She stormed over to the desk, grabbed a bunch of papers, and tossed them outside. Timothy screamed as if Bethany had just thrown a bunch of babies out of the window.

"You monster!"

"This is only the start," said Bethany, scrunching up another pile. "I'm gonna keep throwing them until you promise to get your act together."

"I promise! I promise!" said Timothy. "I had no idea that children couldn't feed themselves, I thought they were just being lazy!"

"Lazy?!" said Bethany. "Are you really standing there

44

and saying –"

She was interrupted by the phone ringing impatiently on Timothy's desk.

Timothy blinked at it. "I've only just put that phone in. How does anyone know the number?" he asked.

Bethany rolled her eyes, as she picked it up. "Look here, Nickle, if you don't give it up, I'm gonna –"

"*Plea– Bethany. Just give me one sentence. One sent– to show why we have to mee–*" pleaded Mr Nickle.

"One sentence, if it'll shut you up. But it better be the last one we ever hear from you," said Bethany.

There was a hiss of silence on the other end of the line. Then, in a slow, deliberate voice, Mr Nickle announced the news he'd been trying to deliver all day.

"*I nee– to speak to you, because the beast has fou–* a way *to escape from its cage,*" he said.

The Wintlorian Warning

In Wintloria, Claudette was struggling. The feasting tree had been evacuated to make her a new home, because she was too weak to fly to her own part of the forest.

Her recovery was being aided by a mixture of science and nature. One of her wings was hooked up to a D.o.R.R.i.S. beeping machine, while the rest of her body was smothered in Wintlorian leaves, bark and fruit foraged by the other parrots. Still, there was something getting in the way of her recovery – something that no Dorris or parrot could understand.

As Mortimer watched Claudette squawk and flap a fretful sleep, he felt helpless. She had been like this, ever since she'd fainted in his wings – neither conscious enough to engage with the world, nor unconscious enough to enjoy the rest she needed.

"Hi-di-hi, Morty! What a devoted little sausage!" said Giulietta, as she swooped into the tree. "You still here then, are you?"

Mortimer had no intention of answering such a stupid question.

"Did you hear me, Morty?" asked Giulietta. Just like all the other parrots in the forest, she was making an excessive effort to remain cheerful in the face of tragedy. "Maybe you're too tired to listen. Shall I get Frederick to fly you up to the tree of restfulness?"

"I'm FINE," said Mortimer, through a gritted beak. He didn't take his eyes off Claudette.

"But you haven't left her side since she got here," said Giulietta. She put a wing around Mortimer. He flinched. The only parrot he allowed to hug him was Claudette. "You must be pooped."

"I'll never leave her," said Mortimer. "Not as long as she needs me."

"What she needs now is rest," said Giulietta. "She has everything she needs to recover."

"I'll scour the forest for fruit that the others have missed.

I'll fly to D.o.R.R.i.S. for a different doctor," said Mortimer. He was speaking to himself more than anyone else, but he still succeeded in offending Agents Hughie, Stewie and Louie, who were fussing around Claudette's bed. "There's got to be something I can do!"

"The only thing we can do is wait," said Giulietta. "If you really won't sleep, then some of us parrots are going to crowd around this tree and sing some cheery lullabies to soothe Claudette. I know you're not much of a singer, but you could add your voice to the choir if you like?"

"A song won't cure Claudette," spat Mortimer.

"A song can soothe the soul and mend the heart. Why, the right song in the right ear can –" began Giulietta.

"A song is clearly no match for the beast!" snapped Mortimer.

Mortimer and the other parrots had been warned not to speak of the beast in front of Claudette. The D.o.R.R.i.S. machine beeped faster and louder than it had ever done before, and Claudette's eyes began to stir with a more disturbing variety of dream.

In times past, Claudette shared her dreams with the young parrots of Wintloria as bedtime stories. If she did that now, none of them would ever sleep again. She kept murmuring words and faces that she had seen in the beast's mind.

"Rapscallicus . . . Morgana . . . BETHANEEE," said Claudette. She slowly blinked herself awake. "What the . . . who the . . .?"

Mortimer flew over to comfort her. Her voice was too weak for him to hear, so he leaned closer to her beak.

"The beast is hungry . . . the beast is always hungry, and its mind is always cunning. Don't let it be cunning, Morty . . . don't let it escape from where it's trapped . . . and, whatever you do, don't let it eat," said Claudette. She was at war with her own exhaustion. "If it eats, it'll eat . . . it'll eat . . . SAVE BETHANY!"

"Who and where is Bethany?" asked Mortimer, as softly as he could. "Claudette? I can't save Bethany unless I know where to find her."

Claudette fell back to her jittery sleep. Mortimer tried giving her a gentle shake, but it didn't work. Mortimer could feel a river of purple tears swimming in his eyelids, but he was determined not to shed a single one

"What did she say?" asked human Agent Hughie.

"Is she in pain?" asked humanish Agent Louie.

"Any clue about what's blocking her recovery?" hissed

not-human-at-all Agent Stewie.

"She keeps talking about someone named Bethany," said Mortimer. "And she said that the beast is going to try and escape. But that's nonsense, isn't it?"

The three Dorrises in the tree looked at each other. Mortimer didn't like the secret conversations that were taking place between their eyes.

"Answer me," snapped Mortimer. "Is there, or is there not, a way of the beast escaping?"

"It wouldn't be able to escape a laser cage . . ." said Agent Hughie.

"Nothing's able to escape our laser cages . . ." said Agent Louie.

"But there's always a way for rapscallions to earn their freedom . . ." hissed Agent Stewie.

Mortimer blinked at the three Dorrises in furious disbelief. The idea of the creature who had hurt his favourite parrot in the world being allowed to roam free made his purple blood boil with rage.

"Tell me everything," he snapped. "NOW."

The Puddle of Chaos

Ebenezer drove home recklessly. He swerved in and out of lanes and honked at every adult, child, puppy and duckie who crossed his path.

"What did Mr Nickle mean, the beast's found a way to escape?" asked Ebenezer.

"How should I know?" said Bethany. "He hung up as soon as he said it!"

Before he even finished parking in the driveway, Bethany scrambled out of the car and sprinted up to her room. She threw jumper after jumper out of her cupboard, until she reached the backpack she had prepared for emergency purposes.

She quickly checked the contents one final time. A

trumpet from the Cussock theatre school, a literally lethal catapult from the Late-Night Pranking Emporium, and a cassette player ready to play a recording of Claudette's cousin Patrick singing 'Hurricane Picnic' (the beast's least favourite song) on repeat. She had also sewn a parachute sheet into the front pocket, in case she needed to jump out of any aeroplanes.

Meanwhile, Ebenezer took a slightly different approach. He didn't have any weapons or secret parachutes to hand, but he had prepared a killer outfit. He unzipped his Special Occasion Uh-Oh Suitbag and slipped on a glossy black turtleneck and a pair of trousers tighter and more fabulous than a ladybird's living room.

They met downstairs, by the front door and put on their wellies. "Where do you think the puddle portal is going to appear?" asked Ebenezer.

"How should I flipping know, you idiot?!" said Bethany. She took a few deep breaths. "Sozza. Bit stressed. He said he was gonna open it somewhere in the house."

"I bet he opens one outside," said Ebenezer.

They ran towards the garden, but, before they even got past the Library of Comic Books and Movies, the whole house started to shake and a puddle grew out of the carpet in front of them. Ebenezer couldn't believe he had got something wrong – *again*. He gulped.

"Ladies first?" he suggested in a warbly voice.

"Fat chance," said Bethany. "We're a team on this."

Ebenezer nodded, and stood on the edge of the puddle with Bethany. They counted backwards from three, and jumped in – disappearing from the garden like two biscuits dropped into a cup of tea. A moment later, they reappeared in the shallow waters that led to the coastline of D.o.R.R.i.S. Island.

Visitors were usually bewitched, bothered and bewildered by D.o.R.R.i.S. Island. They would coo at the fat, high-tech pyramid in its centre and their mouths would drop open at the many species of Dorrises marching ashore from every angle of the sea. They would try to figure out how the water was dry, and they would marvel at the raw, cloudless sun.

Bethany and Ebenezer did none of these things. They were too busy worrying about the beast.

They found Mr Nickle waiting on the beach. The old man's face was jollier than they had ever seen it, and he was being offered pats and congratulations by every Dorris

who passed him.

"Squeezer, Bethany!" cried Mr Nickle in his ragged, jangly voice. He raised his weaponised walking sticks in the air, as if he was welcoming them to a birthday party. "Now then, is there anything I can get you? A tea? Some Martian lemonade? We might even be able to spring for some tears from a dying star, if you fancy something with a kick?"

"The only thing we want is an explanation for what on earth you're talking about," said Ebenezer. "If this is a joke, then it's not a funny one!"

"It's no joke," said Mr Nickle, chuckling good-naturedly. He hobbled up the beach – moving with a pace and nimbleness rarely seen in men of his age. "The beast really has found a way of leaving D.o.R.R.i.S. captivity, and it's extremely good news."

"Good news?!" said Bethany. "Have you gone flipping insane?!"

To make her feelings on the subject crystal clear, Bethany decided she would give Mr Nickle a kick in his stupid shins. She charged at him, but the old man used his sticks to karate–chop her to the floor.

"If you had accepted any of my calls, then I would have had

the chance to explain and guide you into this bally process in a smoother fashion," said Mr Nickle, as Ebenezer helped Bethany back to her feet. "As it is though, we're going to have to do things on the hoof. You'll get your explanation soon enough."

Mr Nickle signed them both into the pyramid, where he received a high five from the blue-faced boy on reception. He received similar attention from several more Dorrises as they walked past the hospital bay.

Bethany and Ebenezer were both dumbfounded. They had only visited the beast here once before, and the atmosphere had been startlingly different. There had been no high fives, and almost everyone had been driven crazy by the mere presence of the beast's rumbling belly upon the island. There also seemed to be lots more fantastical gadgets on display.

Mr Nickle led them to an open elevator. Once inside, he opened the top of one stick to access a control panel, and jabbed the button labelled 'THE CAGE'.

"When we get up there, you might be shocked," said Mr Nickle. "Don't be alarmed if the creature doesn't engage with you right away."

"I won't be alarmed if it doesn't engage with me at all,"

said Bethany. "Mr Nickle, don't do this – *please*."

Whenever Bethany knew she was going to see her nemesis, she felt a gnawing, air-sucking pit of fear just above her belly button. The beast was the only creature in the world who made her want to run away from anything.

"Shouldn't we be wearing helmets?" asked Ebenezer. "I'm sure we were wearing helmets last time."

"Oh no," said Mr Nickle, with a dismissive wave of his sticks. "We haven't needed those for months. Not since the creature's belly quietened down."

The elevator scaled the building in an upward slope. As it approached the final floors, Bethany bunched her hands into fists to try and stop them from shaking. She scrunched her eyes shut, and only opened them when they got to the top.

The top level was different from the rest of the building. The floors were metallic and the walls were lined with the one thing that could kill the beast – trumpets. A human guard was stationed by the elevator, and she seemed remarkably relaxed.

"Come on," said Mr Nickle. "No need to be shy."

Bethany and Ebenezer could both think of several reasons to be shy around the creature whose life mission was to torment and feast upon the rest of the world, but their mouths were too dry to say anything. They stepped further into the room, and saw the beast in its triple-grade laser cage.

The beast was purring in a gentle, snorey sleep. Its three eyes were shut, and its two black tongues were hanging limply on either side of its mouth. There was a look of exquisite peace on its face. But, as Ebenezer and Bethany crept closer, that peaceful expression was replaced with something more wakeful.

The beast's eyes remained shut, but the two black tongues crawled back into the mouth and the nostrils flared with excitement. When it spoke, its voice was still soft, but free from the usual slither.

"Mmmnh, mmnh, mmmmnnnnh! Whatever is that lovely smellsies?" asked the beast.

The Better Kind of Beast

The beast spoke in a babyish voice that neither Bethany nor Ebenezer recognised.

"Smells . . . humany." The beast paused to sniff again. "One of you lovely little humanies smells . . . musty, with just a hint of a word in my head that says 'leather'. Ooh! It's the smell of Nickle-Wickle! But there's another couple of odours here as well. I think I've smelled them before . . ."

The beast peeped an eye open, before quickly snapping open the others.

"OH EMMM GEEEEE! It's Ebby-kneesies and Bethany!" All three of the beast's eyes blinked rapidly, and it sat up. "There's something very, VERY important that I need to say to you. It's something I've wanted to tell you for such a very long time."

Bethany and Ebenezer steeled themselves. The beast

took a deep, stinking breath.

"I just wanted to say . . . sorrykins. SORRY! Not sorrykins, SORRY," said the beast. It slapped itself in the face with both its tongues. "I'm finding it awfully tricky to get my tongues around the words in my blobby head."

When Bethany looked at the beast, all the worst moments of her life were reflected back at her like a malevolent mirror. She had lived this moment several times in her nightmares, but she had never expected it to be like this.

"Still pretending to have lost your mind then?" She tried to sound as confident as possible – knowing from her past that it was a mistake to show even a sliver of weakness in front of the beast.

"There's no pretendsies about it, I'm afraid. All my memmy-wemms are gone. Whooshy-whoosh, bye byesies!" said the beast. It scrunched its blobby face into a Very Serious Expression. "Nickle-Wickle's been telling me all about my horrid past. When he told me about all the things I've done – especially to you, Bethany – I couldn't believey-weave it. Some of the stories made me vommykins. And I'm not talking about the magical kind."

Bethany scowled. She'd been fooled by the beast's tricks before, and she'd promised herself that it would never happen again.

"Oh dear. You don't believe me," said the beast. Its blobby face sagged mournfully. "You still think I'm that beastly beast who did all those dweadful things."

"Probably because you *are* the beast who did those things," said Bethany.

"But I'm not that beasty any more – stinky-promise!" said the beast. "Tell her, Nickle-Wickle!"

Mr Nickle cleared his throat. "The beast is telling the truth. A comprehensive series of brainwave scans has revealed –"

"Not interested in brainwave scans," said Bethany, as she tried to figure out the beast's next move. "I know the truth about the beast. So you can shut it."

"Oh, Bethany – I know you're crossy-woss, but please don't be mean to Nickle-Wickle. He's been ever so good to me," said the beast.

"You're worried about hurting people's *feelings* now, are you?" said Bethany.

"I've changed!" said the beast. "When I learned the truth about myself, I couldn't believe that anyone could do anything so evilicious! It felt like I was hearing about nastinesses done by someone . . . or some*thing*. . . else."

"Are you saying that you're actually feeling . . . regret?" asked Ebenezer in astonishment, stepping closer to the laser cage.

"Don't be fooled, gitface. It's a beastly scheme," said Bethany. She turned back to the beast. "And don't think for one second that we're going to let you get away with it!"

The beast's three black eyes filled with tears of frustration. "But I *have* changed!" it said, stomping one of its tiny feet in frustration. "And I've done it because of you two."

Bethany and Ebenezer looked at each other.

"This should be good," Bethany said.

"I feel a bit embarrassed explaining it," said the beast. It fiddled with its tiny hands and pointed all three eyes in the direction of the floor. "But I kept seeing the two of you in my dreamsies. The more I dreamed of you, the more I wanted to see you. I asked Nickle-Wickle if we could meet, but he said no. He said he would never EVER let me see you again unless I became a good beasty, which I thought was oh-so-meansies."

"Oh-so-wisies, more like," said Bethany.

"I worked at being a good beasty," said the beast earnestly. "First, I learned about my dweadful past. Then, I relearned how to vommykins, so I could make lots of pressies to help

Nickle-Wickle and all his D.o.R.R.i.S. friends."

Bethany looked closely at the beast, trying to find a slip in its performance, something to prove it was the same dribbly stinker that it had always been. So far she could find nothing.

"Satellite chips that never run out of battery, meltproof snow for our ice-cap bases, trampolines powerful enough to bounce astronauts to the moon – the beast has used its vomit to help us with countless missions. You probably saw some of the new gadgets we've got downstairs," explained Mr Nickle. "And most importantly, the beast finally found a way to stop its belly from rumbling."

"What?" asked Ebenezer. It felt bizarre to look at the creature who had tormented him for centuries, and see nothing left of its old personality. "In all the centuries I've known it, the beast's belly has never stopped rumbling. Not even after I brought it a whole colony of bats to eat."

"My belly-welly has been silent ever since Nickle-Wickle said that I had to be a good beasty if I wanted to see you two again," said the beast, giving its belly a pat. "I'm ever so grateful. It's made people feel a lot more comfortable around me."

"There hasn't been so much as a peep out of the belly

for months – and the only thing we've been feeding it is scrap metal," said Mr Nickle proudly. "This creature we've captured may share the beast's body, but it has none of its old personality, and so shares none of the responsibility for its crimes. There was some disagreement from the lower orders, but all the top Dorrises agreed that it would be an injustice to keep it imprisoned."

"Wh-what do you mean?" asked Ebenezer. "Why have you brought us here, Mr Nickle?"

"Ooooaaah! Don't they knowsies?" asked the beast. It clapped its tongues together and wiggled with excitement. "How THWILLING!"

Mr Nickle hobbled across the room to the beast's laser cage. There was a wide, crinkly smile across his face.

"D.o.R.R.i.S.'s most important mission has come to an end," he said. "Today, we are releasing the beast on grounds of extremely good behaviour."

Ebenezer's mouth dropped open in horror.

"You what?!" said Bethany.

"You haven't told them the most exciting bit yet, Nickle-Wickle!" said the beast. "Tell them, TELL THEMMMM!"

Mr Nickle cleared his throat.

"The reason we've called you here today is because we

are releasing the beast into your care," he said. "We want you to help with the final stage of the beast's rehabilitation. In short, we're asking you to show the beast how to be a do-gooder."

"Do you know what this means, besties?" asked the beast in excitement. "It means that I'm coming homesies!"

The Reluctant
Beastkeepers

"Okey bally dokey, let's get going," Mr Nickle said to the guard, pointing at the cage's control panel with one of his sticks. "Time to shut down the laser walls."

The beast clapped its tongues together in delight. Bethany and Ebenezer did no clapping whatsoever, because they both felt like they had been told the unfunniest joke in the world.

"As we shut down the walls of the laser cage, we need you to remain completely still," Mr Nickle said to the beast. "Don't make any sudden movements, and don't step outside the cage, until I say so."

The old man nodded at the guard, who shut down the first of the laser cage's four walls. A few moments later she shut down the second.

"Look at my besties, Nickle-Wickle – they're speechless with excitement!" said the beast. It smiled a dribbly smile as the guard shut down the third wall. "Oh, I am gladsies. I was ever so worried."

The beast's face was the picture of sincerity. It looked like butter wouldn't melt on its tongues, even though Ebenezer knew for a fact that several things much worse than butter had been in its mouth.

He looked over at Bethany, trying to decipher what

she was thinking about all this. He'd half expected her to start kicking Mr Nickle's shins, but she just stood there, motionless – her hands still bunched into fists, and her mouth closed tighter than a wrench.

"I told you not to move!" barked Mr Nickle. The beast was wobbling on its little legs. If Ebenezer hadn't known it so well, he would have said that the beast was wobbling out of nervousness. He also spotted a pair of small D.o.R.R.i.S. wellies on its feet.

Unfortunately, being shouted at did nothing to settle the beast's nerves. Its little legs wobbled even more, as the final wall of its cage was shut down.

"OK – step out slowly now," said Mr Nickle – coaxing the beast with one of his sticks.

It took a while before the beast felt strong enough to take its first step out into the wild. When it did so, it fell flat on its face, and a nail from the metallic floors got jammed in one of its eyes.

"Owwwsies!"

The beast pulled the nail out, and licked its eye until the cut healed. It climbed back to its feet. It was still a little shaky, so it held out its tiny, sticky hands for help, which it received in the form of one of Mr Nickle's sticks.

The beast looked pitiful – so completely removed from the petrifying presence Ebenezer had experienced over the centuries that his brain could barely believe his eyes.

"I'm so excited to become a do-goodinger!" said the beast. It pointed two eyes at Ebenezer and the third at Bethany. "So what do you thinkywink? Will you helpsies?"

Over the centuries, Ebenezer had wondered what it would be like if he could persuade the beast to vomit out an occasional dribble of good into the world. He had long ago abandoned any hope of it actually happening. He looked at Bethany, but she was still silent – as if comatose by the shock of it all.

"I think . . . I have a question for Mr Nickle," said Ebenezer. He turned to the old man. "I just wanted to know . . . when did you start being a nincompoop?"

The joyful expression that had been on Mr Nickle's face all day gave way to a far less friendly arrangement of wrinkles. "I am NOT a nincompoop," he said. "I'm the head agent of the world's most powerful secret agency."

"Okey dokey. Then you're a nincompoop with a fancy title," said Ebenezer. "Because I can tell you now that there's not an ounce of good in the beast's whole body. I should know better than anyone. I lived with it for five centuries."

"Actually, Squeezer, I think you'll find that *we* know the beast better than anyone," said Mr Nickle. He hobbled towards Ebenezer so he could have the pleasure of jabbing him with one of his sticks. "We have records about what the beast was up to long before it even came into contact with you. We know that the beast used to be cruel and cunning and incapable of changing its ways. We know that nothing made it smile more than the misfortune of another, and that it never helped another soul."

"Oh botherkins, stop talking about what I was like before I lost my memmies," said the beast. "It makes me feel so horrid."

"So you know all that about the beast, but you still think it's a good idea to let it on the loose?" said Ebenezer.

"You'll notice I used the *past* tense," said Mr Nickle, jabbing Ebenezer again. "The old beast died when its memories all vanished. This is something new, and we've done every test at our disposal to confirm it."

"Whatever tests you've got, the beast can beat them," said Ebenezer. He softened his tone to one which was far more pleading. "Don't do this, *please*. You have no idea of the chaos you're unleashing."

"I think you'll find I know *exactly* what I'm doing," said

Mr Nickle. "The beast is being released from its cage, today. And one way or another, you two are going to help me with the next stage of its rehabilitation."

Mr Nickle fiddled with the tops of one of his sticks, summoning a huge puddle out of the floor. The hissing, spitting waters wrapped themselves around the feet of Mr Nickle and the beast. Ebenezer tried running away from it, but Bethany just stood still – as if resigned to her fate.

When he saw this, he stopped running as well.

"Mr Nickle, you ca–" he began.

The puddle swallowed them up and spat them across the world. A moment later they popped out in the attic of the fifteen-storey house.

"–n't do this!" Ebenezer finished.

It was a peculiar sensation to start a sentence on one continent and finish it on another. Ebenezer didn't have

time to dwell on it for long though, because there were bigger problems upon his plate.

"Oofywoof! That ride was terribly bumpykins," said the beast. It cast its three eyes in different directions around the attic, and a dribbly smile spread across its lips. "Oh my goshykins . . . I never thought this day would come."

"This day hasn't come!" said Ebenezer. "Send it back, Mr Nickle. You're dooming everyone in this neighbourhood."

"We haven't taken this decision lightly," said Mr Nickle. "It'll all make more sense once you've spent more time with the new beast yourselves."

"That's never going to happen. This whole memory-loss act is just part of some evil scheme, can't you see?" said Ebenezer.

"There is no evil schemesies!" said the beast, looking genuinely distressed by the accusation.

"We can't stop you from releasing the beast from the cage, but we can ask you to remove the beast from this house," said Ebenezer. For the first time in many months, he felt like he might have actually done something useful. He looked over at Bethany, but even the journey across the world hadn't done anything to stop the whole silent dead-eyed thing she had going on. "It's my house, and the fact of the matter is that the beast isn't welcome here."

"This really isn't how I wanted to play things," said Mr Nickle. He rubbed his eyes with one of his sticks, as if he were being forced to babysit a misbehaving toddler. "But you haven't left me with any other option. I am officially ordering you to help with this D.o.R.R.i.S. mission."

"Nice try, but you can't order us around in our own home," said Ebenezer.

"Oh, can't I?" asked Mr Nickle. "Would you be kind enough to inform me how you've managed to live in this very large house for so very long, Ebenezer? Because I checked your records, and I don't believe you've ever had a job."

"Well, I just use the money in the safe. The beast vomited me out bags of the stuff a few years ago," said Ebenezer. "It was a reward for bringing it the throne of Atlantis to nibble upon."

Mr Nickle's eyes gleamed. "So you're saying that the beast's money pays for everything? In my books, that makes the beast the real owner of this house."

The beast gasped a stinky gasp of delight. "Are you saying that I own this homesies?" it asked. "Oh wowzies! How lucky am I?!"

"You can't just –" began Ebenezer.

79

"And there's one more thing," said Mr Nickle. He fumbled through his tissue-laden pockets before producing an official-looking document, which he handed to Ebenezer. "If you refuse to help, then I'll have no qualms in using this."

Ebenezer glanced at the document, with Bethany peering over his shoulder. It took him a moment to realise what he was holding.

WARRANT FOR THE ARREST OF EBENEZER TWEEZER

To all D.o.R.R.i.S. agents in the known universe, you are commanded to arrest the individual named above, on grounds of aiding and concealing the rapscallion known as 'the beast' for over five centuries.

Verdict: Guilty, without trial.
Sentence: Imprisonment by laser cage.

"B-b-but I wouldn't last five minutes in a laser cage!" said Ebenezer. "I'd look awful in a prison jumpsuit. You can't do that to me!"

"I can and I will," said Mr Nickle. "I like you, Squeezer – but there's nothing I won't do to see the beast become a fully redeemed rapscallion. This mission is too important to D.o.R.R.i.S. for me to show any hesitation."

Ebenezer felt in dire need of a good sit–down. He put his head in his hands. It seemed to be getting heavier by the minute – probably from all the thoughts and worries springing up inside his brain.

"Poor ickle Ebby-kneesies," said the beast. "Don't do this to him, Nickle-Wickle. Surely there's another waysies?"

"I've bally had enough of people questioning my judgement. This is the only waysies. I mean, way," said Mr Nickle. "Ebenezer and Bethany WILL help you become a useful part of this world, whether they like it or not."

Ebenezer looked up at Bethany. Her face was stonier than a pebble beach. "It looks like we're going to have to help the beast," he said. A little part of him was intrigued about what this might look like.

Mr Nickle smiled with grim satisfaction, while the beast's face was filled with excitement. Bethany was silent for a few moments. She turned her stony face to Ebenezer.

"No," she said in a quiet voice.

"Come again?" said Mr Nickle.

"I said, *no.*" Bethany swivelled on her sneakers, and started stomping over to the rickety old door. "I'll never help the beast."

"Bethany? Oh bothersies, Bethany, please don't gooo!" cried the beast. "Come back – pleasies! I was so looking forward to getting a chance to know you, Bethany."

Bethany stopped stomping. She turned back round to face the beast.

"You wanna play this weird game? Fine then," she said. "I am your worst nightmare. I'm the person who stopped your evil schemes, twice. And I'm gonna stop you again – even if it means Ebenezer has to go to prison. By the time I'm through with you, you'll be back in that cage, rotting slowly to death. You wanna know who Bethany is? Well, you're looking right at her."

The Long Night

Bethany stomped out of the attic, and slammed the rickety old door behind her. Ebenezer's blinked at the door. Then, he quickly chased after her.

"Get back this instant," barked Mr Nickle. "That's an order!"

"Oh botherkins. Don't gooooo!" cried the beast.

As he left the attic, Ebenezer glanced back and caught a look on the beast's face that had completely taken him by surprise. The beast hadn't looked angry at Bethany's words, it had just looked devastated.

Ebenezer reminded himself that it was probably all part of some evil scheme. He sprinted down the many flights of stairs after Bethany, struggling to keep up – and wondering what on earth she had planned.

"Have you got something I've missed?" he asked, as he panted down the penultimate staircase. "Because it seems to me that the beast and Mr Nickle have us pretty much beat."

"The beast never has me beat," said Bethany. "I'm never gonna let it win again."

She took the final staircase by sliding down the banister. When Ebenezer got there, a puddle was emerging in front of the front door. A moment later, Mr Nickle popped out.

"What in the name of D.o.R.R.i.S. do you think you're bally well doing?" asked Mr Nickle. "Didn't you hear what I said upstairs?"

"Oh, I heard it all. And I reckon . . . I don't have to do anything," said Bethany. "Ebenezer's the only one you can throw in jail. And I'd rather be kicked out of this house than help that thing upstairs. Heck – I'll go back to the orphanage, if it means not spending another moment with that creature. So when it comes to making me do things, Nickle – you've got nothing."

"But Bethany, you've got to help," said Ebenezer, laughing nervously. "I don't want to go to prison."

"I will do it. I'm not bluffing," said Mr Nickle.

"Neither am I," said Bethany, shrugging. "Sozza, gitface, but that's your problem to deal with – not mine."

Bethany grabbed her scooter from the hallway and stomped out of the front door. She heard Ebenezer desperately calling her name, but she didn't turn back.

"Insolent child!" said Mr Nickle. He started fiddling with the tops of his sticks. "She can't just run away from D.o.R.R.i.S.. I'll track her down."

"No, don't!" said Ebenezer. "Just let her get it out of her system. Whenever she's angry she takes to her scooter. She'll be back, I'm sure of it."

Ebenezer plugged the phone back in, just in case she called. He walked into the front sitting room, and took a window seat, so that he would be able to see her as soon as she came back. He was sure he wouldn't have to wait for long.

"Don't think you're right about that," said Mr Nickle, as he hobbled into the room. "That look on her face as she stormed out – I've seen it before. It's normally on the faces of rapscallions who decide they are going to try and make a run for it."

"Bethany doesn't run away from things," said Ebenezer.

He readjusted his armchair so he could see more of the road that led to the fifteen-storey house. "And she doesn't abandon people."

Mr Nickle sighed as he slumped into the armchair on the other side of the window.

"I hope you know her as well as you think you do. Because she's right – if she doesn't agree to help, then there's nothing I can do to force her," he said. "And no offence, but I was kind of counting on her to do most of the work. She seems a lot better on this do-gooding side of things."

"You know 'no offence' isn't some sort of magical phrase," snapped Ebenezer. "I'm very much offended, thank you very much."

"So you think you can help the beast be good?" asked Mr Nickle.

"No, I think the whole idea is a waste of time," said Ebenezer. "But if it was possible to tame the beast, then I'd be just as good at it as Bethany. My problem-solving business has just hit ... well, a few problems ... that's all."

"Well, I hope you're right," said Mr Nickle. "Because the fate of D.o.R.R.i.S. may depend on it."

"No, it won't," said Ebenezer. "Bethany will be back

any moment now. An hour tops – if she's not, I'll eat my trousers."

An hour came and went. Then another, and then one more after that. Fortunately, Mr Nickle didn't hold Ebenezer to his trouser-eating promise.

"Time to face facts, Squeezer. She's not coming back," said Mr Nickle. He stood up and used his sticks to crack his back in a dozen different places. "And I need to get back to D.o.R.R.i.S."

"What?!" said Ebenezer. "You can't just leave me alone with the beast!"

"That's exactly what I'm doing," said Mr Nickle. "Normally, as soon as the rapscallions are released from their cages, D.o.R.R.i.S. interference ends. But, due to the importance of the beast, I'll check in with you more regularly. I'll visit in a few days to monitor your progress."

"A few days?! The beast could have eaten half the neighbourhood by then!" said Ebenezer.

"That's not going to happen," said Mr Nickle. He sighed, and rummaged through his pockets, before producing a thumb-sized button. "But if for any reason I'm wrong about the beast, just click this button and I'll puddle over straight away. All you've got to do is find a way of making the beast a helpful part of society. There's nothing to worry about."

There was so much to worry about that Ebenezer didn't even know how to begin. Eventually, the only thing that came out was –

"Stay with me – just for a little bit longer," he begged. "Just wait with me, until Bethany gets back."

"Bethany's not coming back. Certainly not tonight anyway," said Mr Nickle. "You look exhausted. Time to get some shut-eye."

Ebenezer looked out of the window again – hoping and half expecting to see Bethany's scowly face arriving on the scooter – but all he saw was a dark, empty road. He hated the thought of sleeping in the house without Bethany, because they hadn't spent a night apart since she'd moved in.

"Please, Mr Nickle," begged Ebenezer. He was so tired that his speech was starting to slur. "She will be back, I know it. We're a team on this. We're always a team."

Mr Nickle looked at Ebenezer, with pity etched across his wrinkly face. He hobbled back to the chair and took a seat.

"I'll stay until you fall asleep," said Mr Nickle.

"I'm not going to fall asleep," said Ebenezer, his head already drooping, like a tired puppy. "I'm going to wait for Bethany. She won't . . . she won't abandon me. We're a team. We're a very . . . very . . . good . . ."

And with this, Ebenezer fell head first into the land of nod. Mr Nickle threw a nearby blanket over him, and then opened up a puddle back to D.o.R.R.i.S.

The Sweet-Shop Sleepover

Bethany hadn't left the house with any kind of plan. She'd done it because she needed the space.

Usually, she found scooting around the neighbourhood at night a pretty awesome way to clear her head. But before she even made it to the end of their road, she was waved to a stop by her neighbour, Eduardo Barnacle – a nosy child in every sense of the word.

"What do you want, Barnacle?" she asked.

"A softer tone of voice wouldn't go amiss," said Eduardo, as he flared his humongous nostrils snootily. "Especially as I wish to wish you my most jubilant congratulations."

"You what?" said Bethany.

"Jubilant. It means triumphant and joyous. I learned it from my word-of-the-day loo paper," said Eduardo, enormously pleased to have an opportunity to trot out the new word. "I heard the news about your party! My family were honoured and positively *jubilated* to receive the invitation from Miss Muddle this morning."

"Oh right, that – yeah," mumbled Bethany.

"You don't seem very excited." Eduardo shook his nostrils, and the rest of his head, in a disappointed manner. "If someone was throwing me a party, I'd be tickled pink. In fact, I might even go as far to say that I would be feeling –"

Bethany whizzed away on her scooter before Eduardo had the chance to show off his loo-paper word again. She didn't get far before she was stopped again.

"Congratu-bloomin'-lations!" said the bird-keeper, who ran out of his shop with Keith the dove perched on his shoulder. "Who would'a thought it? The girl who used to teach my talking birdies how to say rude words, getting a bleedin' party! Not me. I'll tell you that much!"

Keith the dove usually looked down on humanity and other lesser species, but even he was inclined to coo pleasingly at Bethany.

Bethany was stopped several more times on her

journey. The kindly old lady, who had offered do-gooding advice in the past, shuffled out of her house to offer Bethany a celebratory cough sweet. Paulo the postman said it had been an honour to deliver every one of Miss Muddle's invitations. Even the zoo-keeper lady, who looked remarkably like a lizard, croaked out a few reluctant compliments.

Bethany was beginning to think it had been a lot easier when the neighbourhood thought that she was a prankster, because at least they avoided her back then. She couldn't face any more compliments, so she parked in front of the one place where she thought she might be able to get some peace – the sweet shop.

The lights were on and the door was unlocked. Inside, there was heavy-metal music blaring and rattling from the sweet-shop speakers. Miss Muddle was at a worktop, holding a blowtorch over another variation of the bombastic bubbletrumpets, which reminded Bethany of the beast all over again. She stomped over and turned down the speakers.

"Don't do that!" shouted Miss Muddle. "The bubbletrumpets might be more musical if they can hear some tunes as I apply the finishing touches!"

Bethany turned the music back up, as Miss Muddle blowtorched the final bubbletrumpet of the batch. Then, as soon as she switched off the blowtorch, she removed a freeze-breeze hairdryer from her apron, and started cooling her creations.

"SWITCH OFF THE MUSIC – NOW!" shouted Miss Muddle. "TOO MUCH MUSIC AND THE TRUMPETS MIGHT BECOME *TOO* BOMBASTIC!"

Bethany cut the music. The sweet shop was silent, save for the crackle of the bombastic bubbletrumpets cooling and solidifying. Miss Muddle gave the trumpets a sniff and nodded approvingly.

"I think I've done it," said Miss Muddle. She beckoned Bethany over as she used an extremely sharp knife to carve

off a slice. "If my calculations are correct, then this should be the taste equivalent of hearing a brass band play a jazzy symphony. Go on, give it a go."

Bethany lifted the slice of cooled bubbletrumpet to her mouth. If there was anything that would cheer her up, she felt a treat from Miss Muddle would do it. But the bubbletrumpet was . . . awful. Instead of a jazzy symphony, it was the taste equivalent of a cat scratching a paw down a blackboard. She spat it back out into the nearest bin.

"What?" asked Miss Muddle. "No, no, you must have it wrong. Clearly your tastebuds aren't refined enough yet."

The sweetmaker cut herself a slice of her own creation.

She gave it three thoughtful chews, before she picked up a bin of her own.

"Sweet sherbert herberts, that was awful!" she said, after spitting it out and vigorously licking a lemon-drop lollipop to get rid of the taste. "Maybe I should have played them some Louis Armstrong instead. They are going to need a LOT of work, if I'm going to get them ready in time for your party." She looked at Bethany in surprise. "What are you doing here anyway? It's not morning already, is it? I do lose track of the hours when I'm sweet-making."

"Nah, it's night all right," said Bethany. "In fact, it's shaping up to be one of the worst nights of my life."

"Oh no, what's wrong?" asked Miss Muddle. "Want to talk about it?"

"Not really," said Bethany. She didn't like talking about her problems with anyone – even Ebenezer. "Sozza, Muddle – shouldn't be bothering you with this. I'll leave you be."

"Nonsense!" said Miss Muddle. She ran over to the door, locked it, and turned the sign from 'OPEN' to 'CLOSED'. "You're going to take a seat, and you're not going to move your bottom one inch, until we've cheered you up."

Bethany was never normally very good at doing what she'd been told. But on this occasion, she was more than happy to follow Miss Muddle's orders. She obediently kept her bottom entirely motionless, as Miss Muddle ran around the shop, collecting a curious assortment of ingredients.

"The cheering up begins with chocolate," said Miss Muddle. She chucked some strawberries, crushed cocoa, full fat cream and something from a box marked 'TOP SECRET' into a heating blender. "A Superdouper Deluxe Muddle Hot Chocolate to be exact. Now I warn you, Bethany, your life will never be the same after you've tasted a sip of this."

Aside from the trumpets, Bethany was a big fan of Miss Muddle's creations. She became extremely excited after Miss Muddle brought out the whipped cream and prickly peppermint marshmallows.

"OK, Bethany – final chance for you to walk away," said Miss Muddle, as she brought over a mug of the finished product. "This WILL rock your world. And frankly, I'm not sure you're ready for it."

"Oh, don't you worry, I was BORN ready," said Bethany. "Maybe you're not ready to hear that your hot chocco isn't as good as you think it is?"

In response, Miss Muddle placed the mug with queenly solemnity in front of Bethany. On a last-minute whim, she added a sparkler into the mountain of whipped cream.

"Here goes . . ." said Bethany.

She took one sip, and her life was indeed changed forever. Her world was rocked and her whole outlook on food and beverages changed, as she tasted the potion-like mixture that was the perfectly equal combination of zingy, creamy, gloopy and fluffy. She closed her eyes and kept sipping until the whole mug was in her belly.

"Oh wowzas!"

"Don't say I didn't warn you," said Miss Muddle, when Bethany opened her eyes again. "You've given yourself a whipped-cream moustache. Suits you rather well, actually."

Miss Muddle picked up the can of whipped cream and gave herself a charming goatee to match, complete with whipped-cream eyebrows. Bethany laughed so hard that she almost snorted out the entirety of the Superdouper Deluxe Muddle Hot Chocolate.

She only stopped laughing when the trumpet on the counter let out a loud and unhappy tootle. The sight of it reminded Bethany of the beast, and everything that was waiting for her back at the fifteen-storey house.

"What is it?" asked Miss Muddle. She knitted her whipped-cream eyebrows into a worried frown. "I thought

I was cheering you up."

Bethany just wanted a normal, beast-free life, where she could have a hot chocolate with awesome people without worrying about being eaten alive. If she could find a way of getting rid of the beast, then she and Ebenezer would be free forever.

"Bethany?" asked Miss Muddle. "You're worrying me."

Bethany didn't want to do that. "No need to worry, Muddle," she said. "I was just pranking you. I only pulled a sad face so that you'd make me another hot chocco."

"Ooh, you little bonbon sniffer!" said Miss Muddle. She started preparing another hot chocolate. "Don't do that to me again."

"I won't," said Bethany. "Hey, Muddle – can I sleep here tonight?"

"Absolutely!" said Miss Muddle. "Do you want to use the phone over there to let Ebenezer know?"

Bethany walked over to the candy-cane phone, and picked it up. There was no answer so she left a message. She considered calling again, but didn't. She was determined to have one more good night, without having to think about the beast again.

"Sure you're OK to stay?" asked Miss Muddle.

"Yeah, course," said Bethany. "What's the worst that could happen?"

The Rude Awakening

Ebenezer woke up to find that Mr Nickle had left, and that Bethany had still not returned. There was also a strange ringing in his ears.

He threw off the blanket and gave himself an almighty head rush by jumping to his feet. He quickly dashed around the ground floor of the house, looking for Bethany in every room, from the Exotic Tea Pantry to the Groovy Disco Lounge. He was about to look on the upper floors as well when he noticed that the answerphone was flashing. He jabbed the play button so hard that he clicked his finger.

"*Oi, oi, gitface!*"

Ebenezer heaved a sigh of relief. He felt certain that Bethany had been working on some brilliant way to defeat the beast's evil scheme.

"Muddle thought I should let you know that I'm staying here tonight. Anyway, you and Nickle have got it all covered. Might give you a call again later, might not."

For a few moments, Ebenezer stood in front of the phone, looking like he had been slapped across the face by a large and deeply unfriendly fish.

He clicked the play button again. There were no other new messages.

He couldn't believe that she would just leave him to deal with the beast on his own. By not helping him, she was basically condemning him to life in a cage. He couldn't remember a time in all his five centuries when he had ever felt more betrayed.

On top of that, the blasted ringing in his ears was growing louder and louder. He tried clearing the sound by jabbing his fingers in and out of the ears, but nothing worked.

He soon realised that the ringing wasn't coming from his ears. It was coming from the very top of the house.

Ebenezer was all on his own with the beast.

Ebenezer patted the button that Mr Nickle had given

him and marched up the many staircases. He barged through the rickety old door and found the beast excitedly tugging on the bell that was beside the red velvet curtains.

"Look at this, Ebby-kneesies! It's fabbywabby!" said the beast. It seemed utterly delighted by the sound the bell was making, like a kitty cat with a brand-new toy.

"Don't act like you haven't seen it before," said Ebenezer curtly. "You always ring it when you want me."

"Are you telling me that this little bellsies lets me have

chatty-wats with you whenever I like?" asked the beast, letting out a stinky gasp. "Well, now it's even MORE fabbywabby!"

Ebenezer didn't have time for this. He wanted to vent his fury at Bethany by commissioning an artist to paint an extremely moody portrait of him in the Posing Gallery.

The beast started ringing the bell again, giggling like a little child. "Every house should have an Ebby-kneesies bellsies!" said the beast. "What sort of things did we used to chatty-wat about, back when I had all my memmies?"

"I'm not playing this game with you," said Ebenezer.

"I just want to know more about what our friendship used to be like," said the beast, tugging happily at the bell again.

"It wasn't a friendship," snapped Ebenezer. His mind was already bursting with outfit ideas for his moody portrait. He thought a leather jacket, and his most bad-boy bow tie might be the perfect choice. "You just ordered me to bring all manner of disgusting meals to this attic."

The beast stopped playing with the bell, and looked at it with a whole new expression.

"Oh dearsies," said the beast. "That doesn't seem like a very friendly thing to do."

"No, it wasn't," said Ebenezer. "Friendship isn't about ordering people to do things. It's about complimenting each other's pretty outfits, and being there to support their unfairly judged problem-solving businesses. It's about being there for each other, and . . . and . . ."

Ebenezer realised that Bethany – his only friend in the world – wasn't being much of a friend to him right now.

"Oh dearsies, I can see that I've made you upset," said the beast. Its blobby face drooped with misery. "Sorrykins. I prommy-wom that I won't ring this bellsies again."

Ebenezer felt the same thing that he had experienced last time he had looked at the beast. Namely, that he didn't recognise it.

The old beast never expressed regrets, unless it happened to be in relation to some ancient species that it had failed to eat. It never cared about feelings, unless it could use the feelings to better season its meals. Ebenezer had to constantly remind himself that the whole thing was almost certainly an act.

"I guess all I want is . . . to be a good beasty," said the beast. "I know you didn't like it when Nickle-Wickle asked you before – but I don't suppose there's any way in the world that you can show me how?"

Ebenezer began to waver. He might discover the beast's plan faster, if he went along with what it wanted.

"Nickle-Wickle seemed most serious about putting you in that cagey-wage," added the beast. "And I think you were rightsies. You wouldn't last five minnywins!"

"Is that a threat?" asked Ebenezer. He raised himself on to the top of his tippy-toes to show how he was not the sort of man who could be threatened.

"Heavens, nosies!" said the beast. The look on its face suggested that it was truly appalled by the suggestion. "I'm just trying to be helpful. Forget I said anything."

Ebenezer began to wonder whether it might be better to at least *pretend* to help the beast. If he found a safe way of taking the beast around the neighbourhood, then he could show Mr Nickle that he had tried – and maybe find a way to stay out of the laser cage.

"What do you think, Ebby-kneesies?" asked the beast. "Aren't you even an *ickle* bit intrigued about the good we could do together?"

The Warlike Wintlorian

In Wintloria, Mortimer was preparing for a dangerous mission of his own. He had no idea where the beast or the Bethany lived, but he was determined to scour the earth – even if it took the rest of his life.

"Why are you sharpening your talons, Morty?" asked Giulietta. She swooped down while he was grinding his talons against a rock on the edge of the forest. "Make them any sharper and you'll turn them into a set of daggers, what-what!"

The trickiest part of Mortimer's journey was getting out of the forest undetected. So he had come up with a rather cunning lie.

"I'm about to leave the forest to go shopping, and I want to make sure my talons are strong enough to carry everything I need," said Mortimer.

"Ooh! What are you shopping for?" asked Giulietta.

"Haven't you heard?" said Mortimer. "I've decided to get a feast ready for Claudette. You know, for when she gets better. I've told some of the other parrots already."

"Great heavens, this is the most spiffy-whiff news I've ever heard!" said Giulietta. "No need to go shopping, though – we can get by on what we have in the forest."

"Not for the sort of feast I have in mind," said Mortimer.

"How exciting! I'll come with you to help," said Giulietta.

"No!" snapped Mortimer. Then, realising he didn't want her to be suspicious, he spoke in a softer voice. "I mean, *no*. I need to do this on my own – it's important to me."

Giulietta suppressed her every natural instinct to force her help on others and nodded her feathery head. She was thrilled to see him finally getting into the feasting spirit. "Well, I think this is wonderful. I understand now why she has been so frightfully keen to speak to you."

"Who's been?" asked Mortimer.

"Haven't you heard, Morty?" asked Giulietta. "Gosh, you must have been out here talon-sharpening for a very long time indeed. Claudette's awake! And she is most keen to have a little chatty-woos."

Mortimer couldn't believe his ears. He jumped off the rock and flew away from the conversation without uttering so much as a *ta-ta*, *cheerio*, or any of the other popular farewells.

When he got to the feasting tree, Claudette was sitting up in bed. She still looked frail and thin, but at least she was awake. She murmured something, but her voice was too weak for him to hear, so he flew his ears closer.

"Morty . . . I heard about the feast. And I just wanted to say . . . thank you," she whispered. *"I'm sure I'll be well enough for it . . . any day now."*

Mortimer felt terrible. He hadn't thought she'd be awake to hear the lie about the feast, and he hated the thought of deceiving her.

"There was something else as well. What I said about the girl Bethany . . . I was delirious. Ignore me. That's not . . . your problem," whispered Claudette. *"D.o.R.R.i.S. have the beast in a cage anyway."*

"Don't worry," said Mortimer. He decided not to tell her about what she had learned from agents Hughie, Louie and Stewie. "What the beast did to you won't ever happen to anyone else. I promise you."

While Mortimer had been out sharpening his talons, D.o.R.R.i.S. had puddled over the small suitcase of things that Claudette had left in the hospital bay. The other parrots had hung the contents of the suitcase in the tree to cheer her up.

Now the branches around her bed were plastered with memories from all the places Claudette had visited. There was a picture of her in Las Vegas, singing backstage with Elvis and her dearly departed cousin Patrick. There were postcards and thank-you letters from the many friends she had made across the world. There were seashells from her favourite beaches and menus from her favourite restaurants; and there were framed black and white photographs of her parents – who, like Mortimer's, had fallen into the hands of trophy hunters. Mortimer watched as Claudette looked at the branches sadly – as if knowing that she would never be strong enough to leave Wintloria again.

Just above Claudette's head, Mortimer spotted a picture postcard of a girl outside a sweet shop. The girl was carrying a backpack with her name on it. Mortimer plucked it from the branch.

"That's Bethany . . . after her first full day at Miss Muddle's

sweet shop. *Such a poppet. Gets a little lost sometimes, but always means well,*" said Claudette.

"I wish you hadn't met her," said Mortimer. "I wish you'd never left this forest to go to that stupid neighbourhood."

"*Don't say that, Morty,*" said Claudette. "*I wouldn't trade my friendship with Bethany for the world . . . even after everything that's happened. I hope you get to meet her one day.*"

Mortimer turned the postcard around. Bethany had left her address on the back.

"Oh yes," said Mortimer. Finally, he had the one piece of information that the Dorrises hadn't given him. "I have a feeling that Bethany and I will be meeting each other very soon."

"*Will you sit with me for a while, Morty . . . while I sleep?*" asked Claudette.

Her head drooped, and faint snores started to pour from her beak.

Mortimer perched at the end of her bed, feeling uncomfortable. If another parrot was in his position, he felt sure that they would sing some sort of soothing song for Claudette.

He opened his beak, preparing to sing, before snapping it shut again. He decided he was not the sort of parrot to sit and sing. He was the sort of parrot to take revenge.

Mortimer looked at Bethany's postcard again and memorised her address. Then he pinned the card back to the branch.

"Watch over Claudette, will you, Giulietta?" he said abruptly, on his way out of the tree. "This shopping trip might take a few days . . ."

Then he took to the skies, cutting the air with the urgent flap of his purple wings. He had a long flight ahead of him that might take a couple of days, but it didn't matter, because he was very much looking forward to the destination.

The Very Good Dog

"Don't think that you're getting your own way here," said Ebenezer that morning, as he held open the rickety old door. "One little trip around the neighbourhood, and then we're bringing you straight back to this attic."

"Thank you sooo much, Ebby-kneesies!" The beast climbed to its feet. It was still a little shaky, so it held out its tiny, sticky hands. Ebenezer folded his arms and refused to help. "I'm so looking forward to spending the day together.'

With great effort and slowness, the beast waddled out of the attic. "Whoasies! Goshykins!" it said, as its three eyes took in the house. "I don't think I can do all those stairs."

"Yes, you can," snapped Ebenezer. He tried giving the beast a little shove from behind. "The quicker you do it, the quicker we'll be done."

"Hmmykins," said the beast. "I think I might need a little help from my belly."

The beast closed its three black eyes and shut its dribbling mouth. It wiggled its blob of a body from side to side, and let out a deep hum. Then, a moment later, its eyes and mouth snapped open, and it vomited out a huge canoe.

"This'll be much easier," said the beast.

It plopped its body into

the front, and patted for Ebenezer to take one of the many seats behind.

Ebenezer crossed his arms tighter and shook his head. The beast rolled its three eyes.

"You better get in, otherwise I could just whoosh away from you," said the beast. "Isn't it a better idea to keep an eye on me?"

Reluctantly, Ebenezer stepped into the canoe. The beast clapped its tongues together in delight.

"Belty seats on, Ebby-kneesies!" said the beast.

The beast wiggled its fingers and sent the canoe whooshing down the many flights of stairs, at roughly the speed of a cheetah who's just realised that they're late for their best friend's birthday party. It brought the canoe to a shuddering halt in the downstairs hallway. The beast jumped

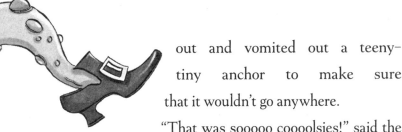

out and vomited out a teeny-tiny anchor to make sure that it wouldn't go anywhere.

"That was sooooo coooolsies!" said the beast. "I loved hearing you scream with joysies!"

"Those weren't joyful screams," said Ebenezer. He unbuckled his seat belt and got out of the canoe, his legs shaking like overexcited maracas. "They were just screams."

The beast's face fell. "Oh dearsies. I'm really not very good at this do-goodingy, am I? I'm sure I can get better though. Where firstykins? Shall we hit the streeties straight awaysies?"

"Hold on a minute," said Ebenezer. "We're going to need to do something about your appearance. If people get one look of you, we could cause a wave of hysteria."

The beast chewed its tongues thoughtfully. It started to hum and wiggle again.

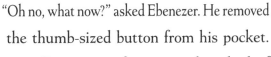

"Oh no, what now?" asked Ebenezer. He removed the thumb-sized button from his pocket.

"I warn you, if you so much as think of

vomiting out any weapons, then I'll . . ."

But the beast didn't vomit out any weapons. It vomited out a large three-piece suit.

"What do you thinksies?" The beast wiggled its fingers and made the suit drape itself around its blobby body. "If I'm going to be a do-gooder like you, then maybe I should dress like you as well? Is this less scary for the neighbourhood?"

Ebenezer knew that he should be focusing on other things, but he couldn't help feeling jealous of the beast's outfit. The pattern of the three-piece happened to be a particularly daring tartan, and Ebenezer felt certain he would look simply marvellous if he was wearing it.

"Much, much worse," said Ebenezer. "Try again."

The beast wiggled its fingers a few more times, and modelled a variety of outfits. It dressed itself as a

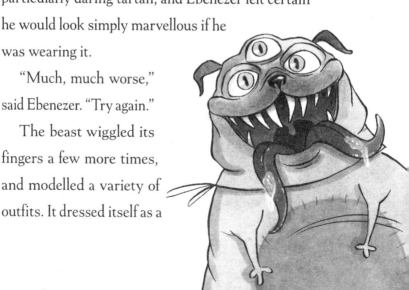

cowboy, a cricketer, a queen and a turtleneck wearer – but nothing seemed to be working. Finally, it wiggled out a dog costume.

"Yes! That's the one. Can you make yourself a hood as well?" asked Ebenezer.

The beast wiggled its fingers to create a hood with eyeholes, which Ebenezer pulled over its head.

"That might do it," said Ebenezer doubtfully. "I'll just tell people that you're my pet. My very ugly, very disgusting pet. You look no worse than some of the dogs I see being walked on these streets."

"I think I could make a great doggy," said the beast. "Let me show you my best barky-wark."

However, before the beast could get any barky-warking done, the doorbell rang.

"Whoever could that be?" asked the beast.

"Got to be Bethany," said Ebenezer. Even though he was still rather cross with her, a part of him was relieved that she had come back to help him with the beast, because he wasn't sure about this dog costume idea at all. "I knew she'd come to her senses!"

"Why would Bethany use the doorbellsies?" said the beast. "Doesn't she live here?"

Annoyingly, Ebenezer had to admit that the beast was right. All his hopefulness disappeared.

The doorbell rang again.

"If this is part of your grand evil scheme, you won't get away with it," said Ebenezer.

"There is NO grand evil schemesies!" said the beast.

Ebenezer tentatively opened the door, just a crack. There was no evil plan lurking on the other side. Instead, there was a Barnacle. An Eduardo Barnacle, to be precise.

"Ah, Mr Tweezer," said Eduardo. "I'm afraid desperation has brought me to your door. I was wondering whether The Wise Tweezer is still operational?"

"Eh?" said Ebenezer.

"Well, you may not remember this, but a week or so I came to you with the problem of my rose bush," said Eduardo. He paused to sadly puff out his nostrils. "The high spot of my day has always been smelling the wonderful bouquets in my rose garden. But recently, a rather odorous new strain of weeds is killing off my poor little pretties. At the time you recommended that I sniffed some rose-scented candles instead."

Ebenezer beamed. "It's nice to see that someone's finally grateful for my work, but I'm afraid I'm a little busy right now –"

"Grateful! I was furious!" said Eduardo, promptly causing Ebenezer's beam to disappear. "I took my problem to the gardening centre. But their top gardener has come back, and apparently even she can't do anything to save them. So I thought I'd try you one final time, Mr Tweezer. Can you think of anything that might help save my one spot of *jubilant* happiness?"

Ebenezer paused for a moment. Then he slammed the door in Eduardo's face – almost chopping off a bit of his nose as he did so.

"What did you do that for?!" asked the beast.

"I have no time for the Contemplation Chambers today," said Ebenezer. He added glumly, "Probably wouldn't be able to help him, even if I had the time."

"But why did he come here in the first place?" asked the beast.

"Because of The Wise Tweezer – my problem-solving business," said Ebenezer. "I thought I could do-good by helping people in the neighbourhood. The only problem is that I'm about as helpful as a woolly jumper in a heatwave."

Ebenezer felt terribly sorry for himself. Everything in his life was turning out to be a failure – and, on top of that, he had the beast to deal with as well.

"So helpsying people with their problems is a way of do-gooding?" asked the beast.

"Yes," said Ebenezer. "But the main problem is that you do actually have to help them."

"Got it, Ebby-kneesies!" said the beast. "I'll get on to it straight awaysies."

"I beg your –" began Ebenezer.

The beast was already back in the canoe and whooshing towards the front door. Ebenezer just about managed to jump out of the way in time as the beast crashed through the door and canoed across the road towards the house with a 'BARNACLE' mailbox.

"Get back here!" shouted Ebenezer.

"CAN'T HEAR YOU!" shouted the beast. "TOO BUSY BEING A VERY GOOD BEASTY!"

The beast canoed around to the Barnacles' back garden. Ebenezer panted and puffed behind – and found Eduardo looking the beast up and down.

"HELLOSIES!" shouted the beast, waving at Eduardo in excitement.

"Mr Tweezer, w-w-what is th-th-that?" asked Eduardo, pointing a shaking hand at the beast.

"Oh, I see where I went wrong. What I meant to say was . . . WOOFSIES!" said the beast.

"It's our pet," said Ebenezer, laughing nervously. He patted the beast's costume-covered head, and tried not to squirm. "We call it the beast. Have you never met a talking pet before?"

"I've heard of them," said Eduardo, trying to recover by speaking quickly and snootily. "It would be very childish not to know anything of talking dogs. What breed is it?"

"Oh, you know – a pretty usual type of breed," said Ebenezer. "Amazingly but definitely *believably* enough, we found it in our back garden. It was so small at first, it got stuck to the bottom of my shoe –"

Ebenezer prattled away while the beast climbed out of the canoe and waddled over to take a look at the rose-bush situation.

"Oh yes, this is easy-sleazy-pig-in-a-breezy," said the beast, nodding to itself. "Stand back, everyone. Woofsies!"

It closed its eyes and started humming and wiggling from side to side.

"Don't you dare vomit out anything evil!" said Ebenezer. He quickly added to Eduardo, "The beast is one of those talking pets who occasionally vomit out evil things – you know the ones, don't you?"

Eduardo nodded, determined not to appear as if he didn't know anything. The beast continued to hum and wiggle. A few moments later it vomited out . . . a gaggle of gardening gnomes.

"That should do it," said the beast, with a satisfied nod at the small, red-hatted gnomes. "As soon as you give these gardening gnomsies a tap on the head, they will get to work – mowing lawns, sweeping leaves, taking care of the nasty, nasty weedies."

"I hope you don't think me ungrateful, but I was actually looking for something that would *improve* my garden, not make it look ridiculous," said Eduardo.

But Ebenezer was worried about things a lot worse than a garden looking ridiculous. He snatched up the gnomes. Perhaps they were secret assassins. Or worse – maybe they contained bombs powerful enough to kaboom the whole neighbourhood to smithereens.

"Sorry, Eduardo," said Ebenezer, smiling weakly. "My bad, bad dog is still in need of some training."

"Nonsense!" said the beast. "My vommywom is lovely."

The beast wiggled its fingers to cause the gnomes to slip out of Ebenezer's hands. Then he gave each of them a

little pat on the head.

"Nooo!" cried Ebenezer. He rugby-tackled Eduardo to the ground, and curled up to protect himself against gnome attacks. "I should never let you out of the house!"

Ebenezer scrunched his eyes shut and put his fingers in his ears. A few moments later, he opened his eyes again – and saw that he had nothing to worry about at all.

The gnomes had come to life and were arguing cheerily about how to solve the problem of Eduardo's overgrown borders. Then they pulled out some tiny gardening tools from their aprons, and started pruning the rose bush with exquisite delicacy and care.

"Look how helpful they are!" said the beast. "Barky-wark, grrrr!"

Ebenezer slowly got to his feet, startled by the evidence that his eyes were presenting to him. The beast had *actually done something to help someone else* – and it didn't seem to want anything in return.

"This neighbourhood was wrong about you, Mr Tweezer," said Eduardo. He blew out a low whistle of admiration through his nostrils and settled on a nearby deckchair to watch the vomit at work. "I'll have to start telling people that you can actually be very helpful indeed!"

This should have been a heart-warming moment for Ebenezer, but it inspired nothing but suspicion. Why on earth was the beast being so kind?

"That was amazing!" said the beast. It climbed back into the canoe, and patted for Ebenezer to join him. "I can't wait to see who we're going to help next!"

Ebenezer looked at the beast. The more time he spent with the creature, the more he began to wonder whether it might really have lost its mind after all.

The Thorny Rose

Bethany woke up late in the sweet shop with the worst sugar hangover in the world, because Miss Muddle had kept bringing her treats throughout the night.

She was surrounded by empty mugs of Superdouper Deluxe Muddle Hot Chocolate, and several empty packets of the top-shelf dark cocoa bars that Miss Muddle only cracked open on special occasions.

"Stinking sugar mice – my head hurts," groaned Miss Muddle.

"Keep it down, Muddle – my ears just can't take loud noises right now," Bethany mumbled.

Bethany lifted her heavy head off a worktop, and saw

yet more evidence of their revelry from the night before. All the messy hot–chocolate equipment had been left out, and there were two broken mixing bowls on the floor from where Bethany and Miss Muddle had used whisks as microphones to sing 'Hurricane Picnic' at one another.

"Jeepers, this place is a tip," said Bethany.

"Don't say that. It's got to be party–ready in forty-eight hours," said Miss Muddle. "The RSVPs have already started coming in, and it looks like pretty much the whole neighbourhood's going to show up to hear how wonderful you are."

Bethany still felt weird about the idea of people coming to the shop to praise her. It was a good kind of weird, though. "Wanna hand clearing it up?" she asked.

"Jingling jelly babies, no!" said Miss Muddle. "We can't have the guest of honour preparing her own party. Not after I've already ruined the surprise for you."

Bethany smirked gratefully, and headed for the door. She had decided that she couldn't run away from her problems any more.

"SEE YA, MUDDLE!" she shouted on her way out.

"Oww, please keep it down," begged Miss Muddle.

Bethany left the chaos of the sweet shop behind her and

scooted back to the fifteen-storey house. She immediately spotted the dog-shaped hole in the door. What the flip had caused that? Climbing through the hole, she was surprised to find that the house was empty.

"GITFACE?" she shouted, as she searched the floors. "NICKLE? . . . BEAST?"

Her first thought was that the beast had eaten everyone and was now hiding somewhere in the house. Before she had time to think another thought, there was a knock at the front door.

Eduardo Barnacle was poking his head through the canoe hole, with a beautiful rose in his mouth. He removed the rose, so he could speak to Bethany.

"I just came to present this to the house," he said, wiggling the rose at her. "It's for your charming doggy. Its gifts have completely cured my weedy woes."

"You what?" said Bethany. "We don't have a dog."

"I think you'll find that you most certainly do," said Eduardo. "Ebenezer brought it round this morning, and he's just taken it on the town. That vomiting trick it does is really most impressive."

"The vomiting what?!" asked Bethany.

"You know the humming and wiggling business. It's much better than anything I've ever seen at the neighbourhood dog show," said Eduardo. "Hasn't Ebenezer showed you?"

Bethany couldn't believe what she was hearing. She was sure that Eduardo must have got it wrong.

"This doggy – did Ebenezer say whether it has a name?" asked Bethany.

"Why of course," said Eduardo, with a nasal laugh. "I think he said it was called . . . the beast."

The Vomit for the
Whole Neighbourhood

"Soooah," said the beast. "Which lucky person are we going to visit next?"

Ebenezer decided to test the beast. He removed a small, leather-bound notebook from his jacket pocket. It contained a record of everyone who had been to visit his Wise Tweezer business.

"Three streets away – second left at the roundabout. The house with the orange door," said Ebenezer. "There's a kindly old lady who needs help delivering a letter."

The beast made the canoe whoosh faster than it had ever whooshed before, making the whole journey a terrifying affair of near crashes and decapitations. By the time they made it to the kindly old lady's house, Ebenezer felt that all 512 years of his existence had flashed past his eyes.

The beast waddled out of the canoe and bashed its tiny fists against the orange door. A few moments later, the kindly old lady opened it, took one look at the beast, and fainted.

"Ooopsicles," said the beast. "Have I killed her, Ebby-kneesies? That's not a very do-goody thing to do, is it?"

"Step aside," said Ebenezer. "I'll handle this."

The beast obediently stepped aside, like the good little doggy it was pretending to be. When Ebenezer got to the kindly old lady's unconscious body, he realised that first aid was one of the many things he knew nothing about.

"Not entirely sure what we should do here," said Ebenezer. He tapped the kindly old lady on the shoulder. "Wakey-wakey?"

The kindly old lady refused to wakey-wakey. Ebenezer frowned, unsure what he should do next. Then he noticed that the kindly old lady was clinging to a letter. He prised it out of her hands.

"This is what she came to me about. She wanted to deliver a birthday card to her granddaughter in Australia, but she feared that she was too late," said Ebenezer. "I thought a simple solution would be to buy a carrier pigeon from the bird shop and give it firm instructions to go to Australia."

"What a fabbywab plan!" said the beast.

"Well, it would have been, if I had bought the right type of pigeon," said Ebenezer. "Unfortunately, the one I got ate the letter and pooped it back out on top of the kindly old lady's best hat. She must have written this one to replace it. I really wasn't much help to her."

"We can fixxy-wix that," said the beast. It closed its eyes, hummed and wiggled a bit from side to side, before vomiting out a post box in the hallway, with a mouth that was constantly opening and closing. It looked positively ravenous for letters. "This boxy will send letters anywhere in the world," said the beast.

The kindly old lady sat up and blinked between Ebenezer and the beast.

"Terribly sorry. Wasn't expecting to see such a peculiar doggy on my doorstep," she said. She looked at the post box. "What's that?"

"Apparently it sends letters anywhere in the world," said Ebenezer. "I'm not sure I'd trust it, if I were you."

The kindly old lady got to her feet, and shuffled across

the hallway to take a closer look at the post box. She waited until the mouth was open, and popped the letter inside. The post box made a chewing sound. Then it burped out a delivery slip. The kindly old lady and Ebenezer looked inside, and saw that the letter was no longer there.

"Mr Tweezer, this is extraordinary," said the kindly old lady. "Thank you so much!"

"It's in Australia now," said the beast shyly.

Unfortunately, the sight of the beast speaking made the kindly old lady faint again.

"I love giving old people helpsies!" said the beast. "And you're absolutely suresies that I haven't killed her?"

"Don't worry, she'll be up on her feet in no time," said Ebenezer. He narrowed his eyes at the beast. "Let's see what else you can do."

Ebenezer made his way through the list of people's problems, constantly on the lookout for any clues that might reveal the beast's evil scheme. For Paulo the postman, the beast vomited out an anti-gravity bag that would make it much easier for him to carry around people's packages and letters. For the milkman, the beast vomited out some unshatterable glass bottles. They even swung by the library, where the beast vomited out some stickers that would allow the books to sort themselves on the shelves. Everywhere they went, the beast seemed nothing short of delighted to have a chance to help people.

"If you really like helping old people," said Ebenezer at last. "I know exactly where we should go next . . ."

Even though he still didn't exactly trust the beast, Ebenezer was hoping that it might be able to vomit out something useful at the retirement home, because Nurse

Mindy had been especially mean about his do-gooding. He was secretly quite enjoying all the praise from the neighbourhood as well.

"You again?" said Nurse Mindy, crossing her arms as Ebenezer and the beast stepped through the door. "And you've brought a smelly dog along as well. How thoughtful."

"WOOFSIES!" said the beast.

Ebenezer suppressed every urge he had to blow a raspberry in Nurse Mindy's face. "We just wanted to see whether you were still having issues with your hearing-aid system," he said.

"As a matter of fact, we are," said Nurse Mindy. "Have you come here to suggest we should use megaphones again?"

Ebenezer trotted out his best fake laugh. "Oh no, we've got something far better than that." He looked over to the beast. "Isn't that right?"

"Are you asking your dog for help?" asked Nurse Mindy. "This really is a new low."

In response, the beast hummed and wiggled, and vomited out . . . a whole new set of hearing aids. The hearing aids were a bit slimy with dribble, but aside from that, they seemed perfect.

"Ewww, that is GROSS!" said Nurse Mindy. "If you

think for one minute that I'm going to let those things anywhere near our residents, then –"

Ebenezer picked up one of the hearing aids and jammed it in the ear of a passing resident – the old showgirl who could still do the splits at the age of eighty-nine.

The showgirl blinked a few times – first in shock, then delight. "This is miraculous!" she said. "I can hear better than I have in years. No, actually – better than I have in my whole life. I can hear conversations taking place two rooms away!"

Ebenezer smiled with extraordinary smugness, while Nurse Mindy frowned. But then the showgirl suddenly looked angry.

"Is something wrong?" asked Nurse Mindy. She fired a glance in Ebenezer's direction, while Ebenezer fired a glance of his own at the beast. "I thought that something like this might happen with Mr Tweezer involved."

"There's nothing wrong with the hearing aid," answered the showgirl. "It's what I can hear people saying about me in the other room. Just wait until I get my hands on that Margaret!"

The showgirl stormed into the residents' lounge, heading straight for the guilty-faced Margaret, while Ebenezer and the beast handed out hearing aids. Many of the residents were disappointed that Ebenezer hadn't brought Bethany.

"Is it just you today?" asked the resident with the moth-eaten jumper. "Where's your friend?"

"Just me, I'm afraid," said Ebenezer. "But I think you'll like the things I've brought."

At first many of the residents were hesitant to try out the dribbly hearing aids. But, one by one, they all had a go. The effect was as immediate as it was emotional, with some of the residents even crying with delight to have their hearing restored in such a sensational fashion.

After months of disappointing the neighbourhood with

the fruits of his Contemplation Chambers, Ebenezer felt pretty great.

"Would it be possible to take a photograph?" asked the showgirl, after she had finished with the now extremely sheepish Margaret.

"Who with this time?" asked Ebenezer, rolling his eyes.

"With you, of course!" said the showgirl. "And your charming dog!"

Ebenezer blushed with delight. He set about pulling all manner of provocative poses, as he took one selfie after another with the beast and the showgirl. Soon everyone else wanted one as well, and Ebenezer was more than happy to oblige.

Even Nurse Mindy had begun to soften towards him. "It seems I owe you an apology, Mr Tweezer. I might have been wrong about you, after all."

"Don't worry – you're probably not the only one who was wrong about someone," said Ebenezer. He looked over at the beast, which was smiling a wild, fangy grin underneath its dog hood – clearly delighted by the sights of merriment that its vomit had brought people. "Sometimes it just takes a little while to realise the truth."

Ebenezer felt enormously pleased with himself as he made

his way to the canoe with the beast. He felt significantly *less* pleased with himself when he saw Bethany zooming towards them on her scooter, with a furious scowl upon her face.

The Battle of Bethany and Ebenezer

"Have you come to help with the do-gooding as well, Bethany?" asked the beast. "This is the best day of my lifesies!"

The fury on Bethany's face suggested that it was not shaping up to be the best day of *her* life. She kept her eyes fixed on Ebenezer as she scooted towards them.

"You might want to slow down a lit–" began Ebenezer.

His helpful advice was cut short by Bethany jumping off her still moving scooter and tackling him to the ground. She pinned him down and started beating him around the head.

"You IDIOT!" she shouted. "You traitor! You dim-witted nincompoop of a buffoon! How could you do this to me? We're supposed to be a team!"

"I'm newsies to all this, but I don't think that's how do-gooding is supposed to work, Bethany. You're hurting poor ickle Ebenezer," said the beast.

Ebenezer pulled Bethany's hair. She kicked him repeatedly where she knew it would hurt most – his beloved waistcoat.

"You're really going to accuse me of being a bad teammate?!" said Ebenezer, as they struggled. "You weren't being very team-minded when you abandoned me last night!"

"It was one night!" said Bethany. "I can't believe you're punishing me by taking the beast around the neighbourhood."

"This isn't me punishing you. This is me trying to save my own skin," panted Ebenezer. He decided not to mention the fact that he was quite enjoying all the praise he was getting from do-gooding with the beast. "If I hadn't done something, I'd probably be in a laser cage by now."

"You'd be better off in a laser cage, if this is the sort of thing you do when I'm not around," said Bethany.

"As a matter of fact, today has been a huge success," said Ebenezer. "We've been do-gooding all over the place. And it's convinced me that Mr Nickle was right! The beast HAS changed!"

Bethany was so appalled by Ebenezer's words that she stopped kicking him. He repaid the favour by releasing her hair.

"You can't be serious?!" she said.

"I've spent more time with the beast than anyone on this planet and, after everything I've seen today, I'm sure that the creature really has changed," said Ebenezer. He climbed to his feet, and checked for signs of damage to his outfit. There's nothing left of the old beast."

"Oh yaaaaysies!" cried the beast.

"So you're not just doing this to get back at me?" asked Bethany. "You really have been tricked by the beast?"

"I haven't been tricked by anyone!" said Ebenezer.

"No tricksies from me," said the beast.

"And once you've spent more time with it, you'll see I'm telling the truth," said Ebenezer.

"That is NEVER gonna happen," said Bethany. "Unlike you, I have a brain."

Ebenezer tightened his cravat and straightened his trousers with what little dignity he could muster. He treated Bethany to his coolest stare.

"Well, that's a shame," said Ebenezer. "Because the

beast and I are going to do some more do-gooding."

"No, you're not!" said Bethany. "I forbid it!"

"You can do no such thing," said Ebenezer. "But you can join us if you like. There's plenty of room in the canoe."

"Oooh, yes! Join us, Bethany, pleasies!" said the beast.

"I'm not gonna just let you keep spreading vomit around the neighbourhood!" said Bethany. "I don't know what the beast's scheme is, but –"

"Come with us to uncover this so-called scheme, if that makes you feel better," said Ebenezer, shrugging. "Either way, the do-gooding is happening."

Ebenezer and the beast got back into the canoe. Bethany refused to sit inside it. She followed them on her scooter instead.

The next destination in Ebenezer's notebook was the orphanage. The beast whooshed the canoe across two honking lanes of traffic, so they could get there as quickly as possible.

"Not the orphanage, Ebenezer!" shouted Bethany. "Think of Geoff– I mean, the children!"

"Don't you worry, I won't eat a single one – stinky-promise!" said the beast. This did very little to reassure Bethany. "I'm a whole new beasty now."

The beast pulled the canoe to a halt inside the crumbling gates. The children were dotted around the barren front lawns, playing with rocks as quietly as possible, because Timothy told them that he needed to focus on his precious paperwork.

At the sight of Bethany, Geoffrey started doing an excited, double-handed, flappy wave. He was waving with so much excitement that it looked like his arm was trying to break free from the rest of the body.

"HULLO-ULLO!" he shouted.

The other children shushed him. They desperately wanted Timothy to finish his paperwork, so that they might have a chance of being fed that evening.

"Oh, ah, sorry, sorry," said Geoffrey. He lowered his voice to a whisper. *"Hullo–ullo, Bethany. Did you get chance to read that comic? Because, like I was saying, there's actually a D.I. Tortoise movie coming out soon, and, oh, ah, well, if you don't have plans I would be –"*

"You what?" shouted Bethany. "I can't hear a flipping word!"

"Shhhhh! Shhhhh!" pleaded the other children again.

Geoffrey ran over. As he ran, he opened and closed his arms, as if unsure about whether or not to give Bethany a hug. In the end, he decided against the whole hugging enterprise, and arrived where Bethany was stood with his hands firmly in his pockets.

"Is that your dog?" he asked. "I love you! Oh, ah, I mean, I love pets!"

"Stay away from that thing, Geoffrey," said Bethany. "It is quite literally a matter of life or death."

The beast waddled over to Geoffrey with a big, dribbly smile across its face. Geoffrey ignored Bethany's pleas, and gave it a pat.

"Ooh, that's just lovelykins," said the beast, as it snuggled into the pat.

"Gosh, this is a very clever animal," said Geoffrey. "Is it a dachshund?"

Bethany shoved Geoffrey away from the beast. He thought she was shoving him away from her, and looked terribly glum.

"Don't pull that face," said Bethany. "I just don't want you to get eaten alive."

The beast started to hum and wiggle. A moment later, it vomited out a collection of dribble-covered toys – including shape-changing Frisbees and skipping ropes that could skip themselves.

"HERE WE GOSIES!" the beast shouted to the children. "Woofy-woof, barrrrk!"

"Nobody touch any of those things!"shouted Bethany.

"We can't leave them playing with rocksies now, can we? That wouldn't be very do-goody!" said the beast.

Bethany tried to confiscate the vomit, but failed miserably. None of the children were going to give up the first actual toys that they had seen in ages. A single tear leaked out of Geoffrey's eye as he threw the first Frisbee he had thrown since his parents had died.

"Look at all these smilies," said the beast, looking pretty close to tears itself. "Isn't it the best thing in the world?"

"What are you gonna do, make the Frisbees turn into axes or something?" asked Bethany.

"Hohohosies, you are a funny one, bestie," said the beast. It sighed with delight at all the happy, laughing children and waddled back to the canoe. "Come on – more do-gooding to do!"

"You better stop with the vomiting," said Bethany. She removed the trumpet from her backpack and waved it menacingly in the beast's face. "Or I'll put a stop to YOU."

"What a pretty thingy-wing," said the beast. It apparently had no idea what the trumpet could do.

Ebenezer and the beast canoed their way around the rest of the neighbourhood, with Bethany keeping a safe distance on her scooter. The beast vomited out luxurious yurts for those at the homeless shelter. At the children's hospital, it vomited out bandages that could snap broken limbs back together.

"Oofsies! I'm exhausted," said the beast, as the canoe slowed down to the pace of a dying donkey. "Do you think we can go homesies and have an ickle break?"

"Not yet," said Ebenezer. He was becoming addicted to all the compliments they were getting. "Just one more stop."

Ebenezer directed the beast to park outside the bird shop, and ran inside ahead of the others. He found the bird-keeper preparing for the end of the day by sweeping away all the feathers from his floor.

"I've come to help you with your smelly hoatzin," announced Ebenezer rather grandly.

"No bleedin' thank you," said the bird-keeper, as he continued to sweep. "I had enough of your bleedin' help the last time. Shops like these don't run themselves, you know."

"Ah, but this time I've got something that I really think you're going to like. And it's the solution to all your stinky birdy woes," said Ebenezer. He ran back to the shop door, swung it open, and announced, "May I introduce you to my charming, talking dog . . . the beast!"

As soon as the beast stepped into the shop, its whole expression changed. Its three black eyes dilated with excitement, and its nostrils flared.Bethany hovered furiously on the pavement.

"I don't care whether it can talk or not, there are no dogs allowed in my shop!" said the bird-keeper. "I've got to protect the poor birdies."

"Don't worry – this dog isn't a biter. And it can do things much more interesting than just talking," said Ebenezer. "Just let us take a closer look at your hoatzin problem. You won't regret it."

Ebenezer beckoned the beast further into the shop. Bethany spotted the look on the beast's face and stepped inside. What on earth was it planning?

The hoatzin was the only bird who was sitting alone. Every time it tried to join a conversation, the other birds hopped and waddled away from its stench.

"Poor hoatzin," said the bird-keeper. "The only thing it wants in the world is a friend, but it'll never get one. At the moment none of the other birdies wanna play with it 'cause it's so stinky. Then it gets sad – and the sadness makes it even stinkier."

"There's no problem The Wise Tweezer can't solve," said Ebenezer. He puffed his chest out, looking vaguely like the puffy-chested magnificent frigate in the cage behind him. "Isn't that right, beast?"

Now that the beast was closer to the birds, its nostrils were flaring even more.

"Oh dearsies," it said in an anxious voice. "I seem to recognise a lot of smellsies in here."

"Just do your thing," hissed Ebenezer. "You're making me look like a fool!"

The beast scrunched its worried eyes shut. It hummed and wiggled – wobbling a little on its feet – before vomiting out a transparent box with a swirly tube sticking out the end of it.

"Well, I've seen some bloomin' strange creatures in my time, but I ain't ever seen anything like this," said the bird-keeper. "What the bleedin' hell is it?"

"Bet it's some sort of bomb," said Bethany.

"It's a stink-box. That tubey-wube will let air in, so the birdy can breathe, and turn the bad odours into sniffalicious ones on their way back out. It's also light enough so that it won't stop the bird from flying about," said the beast. It started fiddling nervously with its tiny hands. "Can we leave now? I really think we should go homesies."

Ebenezer had no intention of leaving until he had been praised.

"Go on, give it a go," he said in excitement.

The bird-keeper picked up the stinky hoatzin and gently placed it in the stink-box. Its foul odours were immediately replaced with sweet-scented ones. And just like the beast said, the stink-box was light enough for the hoatzin to move itself around the place.

The hoatzin used the stink-box to hop towards Keith the dove and the fantastically ferocious eagle. For the first time in its life, it was greeted with merry coos and squawks.

"Look at them go! I ain't ever seen the hoatzin so happy," said the bird-keeper. "Mr Tweezer – you're a bleedin' genius!"

Ebenezer beamed.

"Bestie, I really think we should go," said the beast. It tugged at Ebenezer's sleeve. "I don't think it's safe for me to be around all these smellsies for much longer."

"Hush, hush," said Ebenezer. "I think the bird-keeper

Fluttersbury III

Foul Owl

Scarlet
Poopernelle

Gigi

LL Coo J and
Coo D'Etat

Patrick

Montcrief

was about to say some more nice things about me."

"Too bleedin' right I was," said the bird-keeper, who was almost moved to tears by the sight of the hoatzin's happiness. "Mr Tweezer, you are –"

Unfortunately, the rest of the bird-keeper's sentence was drowned out by a low, thunderous rumble. The rumble was such a loud and horrible sound that it cracked the bird-keeper's shop window, and caused all the birds in the shop to cry out in alarm.

It was the beast's belly.

The Belly of the Beast

This particular rumble of the beast's belly was an awful, scratching sound that echoed in listeners' ears, and caused them to lose track of their thoughts. Bethany, Ebenezer and the bird-keeper were forced to their knees. The birds in the shop continued to squawk, screech, quack and coo in distress.

"Oh no, nosies!" said the beast. "Shhhh, naughty belly. Shh, shh, shushykins!"

The belly continued rumbling. It seemed to be making up for lost time.

"That sound is making my ears bleedin' well bleed!" said the bird-keeper.

"Oh botherkins!" said the beast. "I don't know how to

make it stopsies!"

The beast quickly waddled out of the shop.

Bethany came to her senses. "I knew it!" she said, as she scrambled to her feet and headed in a dazed fashion towards the door. "I knew it was the same old beast! Don't let it escape!"

Ebenezer followed hot on Bethany's sneakers. Outside, the beast was trying to silence its belly by thwacking it with its tiny fists.

"We have to call Nickle!" said Bethany.

"He gave me this in case of an emergency," said Ebenezer, producing the thumb-sized button from his pocket. "But I'm not sure that –"

Bethany snatched the button and pressed it as hard as she could. A moment later, a puddle grew out of the street.

Mr Nickle popped out of it – swishing one of his walking sticks as if it were a sword. He winced at the sound of the beast's belly rumbling.

"What happened?" he asked, turning to Bethany and Ebenezer

"Exactly what I said would happen!" said Bethany. "The beast sniffed a shop full of things it wanted to eat, and its true personality came out. Looks like you're gonna have to put it back in its cage."

"Owwwsies," said the beast. "Don't let my belly do any more damage to Bethany and Ebenezer."

Mr Nickle wrinkled his already wrinkly brow.

"Has the beast had anything to eat today?" asked Mr Nickle.

"I thought you said it didn't eat any more," said Ebenezer.

"It doesn't eat meat, but it still needs to eat, you bally fools!" said Mr Nickle.

He aimed one of his sticks at a spot above the beast, and opened a puddle portal in the air. A few moments later, a mountain of scrap metal fell into the canoe.

The beast excitedly gnawed on the metal, like a dog with a collection of juicy bones. Within the space of ten seconds, the entire mountain was inside its belly. Pretty soon after that, the rumbling shuddered to a halt.

"Oh, thank you so much, Nickle-Wickle!"

Mr Nickle opened another portal filled with metal, just to be sure.

"What are you doing?" asked Bethany. "Don't give it food – give it the cage!"

"Did the creature actually eat any of the birds?" asked Mr Nickle.

"No, but –" began Bethany.

"So you're saying that you took the hungry beast into a room full of animals, and it didn't take so much as a bite? That is most encouraging," said Mr Nickle. "How's the rehabilitation campaign going?"

"Up until now, it was going rather well, actually," said Ebenezer. "It's been vomiting useful things for the neighbourhood all day."

"Good. Very bally good," said Mr Nickle.

"Yes, and I don't wish to tootle my own horn," said Ebenezer, as he prepared to give himself a tootle. "But several of the neighbours have been complimenting me on –"

"Have you two lost the flipping plot?" said Bethany. "The beast proved it hasn't changed! Look at the shop!"

"Better tidy that up," said Mr Nickle. He pointed one of his sticks at the window to seal up the crack. He hobbled into the shop and returned a few moments later. "Little memory wipe for the bird-keeper. He won't remember the rumbling at all. Now then, better get back home."

Mr Nickle opened a puddle in the ground that was big enough to fit the beast, Bethany, the canoe, Ebenezer and the scooter. A moment later they were back in the attic.

"Take the beast back to D.o.R.R.i.S.!" shouted Bethany.

"Please don't, Nickle-Wickle! I've been so enjoying all the do-gooding," said the beast. "And listen, my belly's stopped being crossy-woss!"

"As long as Ebenezer and Bethany keep you fed, I see no reason why you shouldn't be allowed to continue your rehabilitation here," said Mr Nickle. "In fact, your restraint in the bird shop indicates that you're making great progress. Well done, Ebenezer."

Ebenezer blushed. He had received many compliments already, but to get one from Mr Nickle seemed like the prize of the lot.

"IDIOTS!" said Bethany, looking between Ebenezer and Mr Nickle. "What will it take for you to see that this is all part of the beast's evil scheme?"

"Why on earth would it be doing all this do-gooding, if it hasn't really changed?" asked Ebenezer. "If you have an answer, then I'll stop helping the beast immediately."

Bethany opened her mouth, closed it, and opened it again – looking vaguely like a goldfish.

"I don't know, all right? None of it makes any flipping sense," she said. "But I know one thing for certain, and it's that the beast has definitely NOT CHANGED!"

"People said that about you and me. They didn't think

we could become better people, and now look at us," said Ebenezer. "I know that the beast has done some truly unspeakable things, but doesn't it deserve a second chance as well?"

"Nah – don't you dare try and compare me to the beast," said Bethany. "We are nothing alike, do you hear me? NOTHING ALIKE!"

"Well, I've heard all I need," said Mr Nickle. He opened a puddle portal in front of his feet. "Keep up the good work, Squeezer."

Mr Nickle disappeared into the puddle, while Bethany stomped out of the attic, with hot tears in her eyes.

She had been angry with Ebenezer many times before, but she couldn't remember a time when she had felt more furious. After everything they had been through, she couldn't believe that he was comparing her do-gooding transformation to whatever the beast was doing.

"I am nothing like the beast!" she shouted to herself again.

As she shouted, she wondered whether maybe this was the problem. If she really wanted to defeat the beast, then maybe she had to be willing to do all the things that it would do. If she didn't toughen up, then she would never get the better of such a cunning creature.

She used her sleeves to dry her eyes, and, as she did so, an idea flashed in front of her eyes. It was tricky, and potentially incredibly dangerous, but it was the only way.

Bethany decided that she was going to feed the beast.

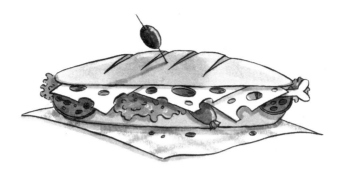

The Sinister Sandwich

Bethany woke up early in the morning, and prepared the meatiest sandwich she had ever made – tearing out the soft innards of a French baguette, and stuffing it with strips of chicken, pork, beef, boar, ox and anything else she could find in the meat fridges. She put some cheese on top to disguise what was inside.

Bethany had hoped to make the sandwich in peace, and sneak it up to the beast nice and early. But before she finished making it, Ebenezer came downstairs. He was dressed in an even sillier outfit than usual, and his face was positively dripping with smugness.

"Good morning!" he said. "Making another peculiar

sandwich? Well, I hope it turns out excellently."

Bethany scowled. She still wasn't anywhere near close to forgiving him.

"What are you doing up so early?" she asked.

"The Wise Tweezer is about to do a record day of business," said Ebenezer. He practically skipped from the kitchen to the front room. "Just look at THIS!"

He drew open the curtains to reveal a huge crowd of people on the front lawn of the fifteen-storey house.

"Isn't it marvellous?" said Ebenezer. "They must have heard about all my do-gooding from yesterday."

"You mean the beast's vomiting," said Bethany.

"Yes, yes – it's the same thing, really. After all, they wouldn't have received any vomit in the first place, if I hadn't been clever enough to take the beast out on tour," said Ebenezer. He turned round and saw that the scowl on Bethany's face had deepened. "Now I know we've had our tiffles, but I really think we should put this whole arguing business behind us. Soon enough you'll see that I'm right on this one."

"Soon enough you'll see what an idiot you've been," said Bethany.

She grabbed her baguette, and headed for the staircase.

However, before she could even take a step, the beast whooshed down in its canoe – still wearing the dog costume.

"Whooopeeeeesies!" it cried, as it wiggled the canoe to a halt in the hallway. "Morning, Bethany, morning, Ebby-kneesies! When can I start vomiting?"

"I'm sure that someone will ring the doorbell any min—" began Ebenezer.

He was going to say 'any minute', but the correct term would have been 'any millisecond', because the doorbell immediately started dingedy-donging.

"Ooh yaysies!" said the beast. "Hurry, bestie, hurry!"

Ebenezer checked himself in the hallway mirror, blushed at how pretty he was looking in his new outfit, and opened the door. As usual, the front of the queue was headed by Eduardo Barnacle.

"The word of the day on my loo paper this morning was *astounding*. A very fitting word, I believe, because I've been truly *astounded* by everything your gardening gnomes have done for my garden," said Eduardo, who had prepared a little speech. "I hope you don't think me greedy, but I was wondering whether you might have anything that might make my garden even prettier?"

Ebenezer shut the door in Eduardo's face and turned to

the beast. The beast vomited out some instant-growing seeds for a flower that could help sniffers rediscover forgotten memories.

"Give these to the gnomes, Eduardo," said Ebenezer, as he re-opened the door. "They should prove a real treat for the nostrils."

"Mr Tweezer, I am *astounded* – you are fast becoming one of the most wonderful people in the neighbourhood," said Eduardo. Then he said something that made Ebenezer grin and Bethany grimace. "If I was Miss Muddle, I'd throw tomorrow's party in honour of you instead."

The next person in the queue was the lady who looked remarkably like a lizard. She wanted to know if there was a way of speaking to the animals she worked with in the zoo.

"Particularly the elephants," she croaked. "I want to have a serious word with them about their bowel movements."

Ebenezer closed the door on her and clicked at the beast. It vomited out a lilac scarf and a matching pair of earmuffs.

"Tell Miss Lizardy to tie the scarf

tight around her neck when she gets to the zoo. The scarf will allow her to talk to the poop machines, and the earmuffs will allow her to listen to them," said the beast. "Ooh, actually, can I give these ones to her? I'd love to have a chance to chatty-wat with the neighbours!"

"No!" blurted Ebenezer. "I think it's best for the whole do-gooding mission if I'm the one to hand out the vomit."

Ebenezer presented the items to the lizard lady.

She furrowed her thin brows in a suspicious frown. "If I put these on in the elephant sanctuary and nothing happens . . ." She proceeded to threaten Ebenezer with a punishment that's far too rude to be printed on these pages. "But if they work, I'll tell all the animals what a wonderfully helpful Tweezer you are."

Ebenezer turned around with glee as the lizard lady left the lawn. "Did you hear that? Even the animals are going to know how wonderful I am!"

Several hours passed like this, with the beast vomiting out an array of marvellous things, while Ebenezer took all the credit. Bethany kept on waiting for the vomit-fest to come to an end, but the crowd outside just grew larger and more impatient. There was no way she could persuade the beast to eat the meaty sandwich while all this fake do-gooding was going on.

At one point, even Miss Muddle turned up.

"I've been hearing all about your remarkable problem-solving pet!" said Miss Muddle. "I don't suppose it's able to cough up anything that might sort out my shop in time for tomorrow? It is definitely NOT party-ready."

Ebenezer closed the door, while the beast vomited out two spidery robots – with metallic boxes for bodies, and snaking tentacles for legs.

"Don't you dare do anything to my Muddle!" snapped Bethany.

"They're spider-tidiers!" said the beast with excitement. It placed the spider-tidiers on the floor and, just like the gardening gnomes, they immediately got to work – tidying the hallway. "I do hope Muddle likes them."

"We're not gonna give her a chance to like them," said Bethany. "Ebenezer, don't pick them up. No, don't you dare open that door and give them to –"

Ebenezer presented the vomit to Miss Muddle.

"Giddy gobstoppers!" she said, gaping at the spider-tidiers. "These look marvellous!"

"Don't take them, Muddle! Whatever you do stay aw–" said Bethany.

Ebenezer silenced her by putting a hand over her mouth.

"Bethany's a little scared around dogs," he said to Miss Muddle. "Don't pay any attention. Those spider-tidiers will have the shop spick and span in no time."

"If they can handle the tidying, that leaves a whole day to work on the bubbletrumpets!" said Miss Muddle. "Thank you so much, Ebenezer!"

Bethany tried to say something but Ebenezer slammed the door, and kept his hand over her mouth, until Miss Muddle left. Bethany eventually got some teeth free and used them to bite Ebenezer's hands.

"Owww!" he said. "I'm bleeding."

Bethany couldn't care less. She stuffed the Nickle-summoning button she had nicked from Ebenezer into her pocket and eyed the beast. "Are you hungry yet?" she said, clutching her sandwich behind her back.

"Oohsies!" said the beast.

"Later," said Ebenezer firmly.

Bethany decided she couldn't stand to watch any more vomit being handed out to the neighbours, so she stomped back up to her room with her sandwich to wait it out.

The waiting it out took a long, long time. The moon was high in the sky before the final person vacated the lawns. Bethany took her sandwich back downstairs again – determined to stop the beast before it could enact any more of its evil scheme.

"Oh deary, bestie – I'm not sure if I'll be able to do much more," the beast said to Ebenezer, as she stomped down the final staircase. "I think I've sprained my tongues."

"Don't worry, that's the last of them," said Ebenezer. "I've just given the train conductor the megaphone that'll make sure none of the passengers can ignore his announcements. He was thrilled."

"Oh goody," said the beast. It did a slow twirl of joy. "Nothing makes me happier than making other people happy."

Bethany rolled her eyes. Ebenezer inspected his watch, and realised how late it was.

"Better get you something to eat," said Ebenezer. "Don't want a repeat of yesterday."

Bethany clutched the sandwich behind her back even

tighter. A repeat of what had happened yesterday was exactly what she had in mind.

"Do you really have some scrappy-wap for me to eat?" asked the beast.

"As a matter of fact, I have some top-drawer metal in the Silverware Suite on the ninth floor," said Ebenezer. "It's very rare and refined. Exactly what you deserve for all your work."

He jogged upstairs to fetch the silverware.

It took Bethany a moment to realise that she had finally got what she needed – time alone with the beast. She knew she had to act fast.

"What did you think of my vommy-womming, Bethany?" asked the beast. It smiled a dribbly smile, and if she didn't know better, she could have mistaken it for one of true kindness.

"Oh yeah – sooo impressive," said Bethany. With her free, non-sandwich-carrying hand, she checked on the trumpet shoved down the back of her trousers, in case she needed to defend herself. She checked the Nickle-summoning button too. "That work must make you very hungry?"

"It does, actually – thanks for asking!" said the beast. It seemed genuinely delighted that she was involving herself in a conversation. "The scrappy-wap will fill me right upsies."

"Wouldn't you like to try some human food?" asked Bethany.

"Nickle-Wickle and D.o.R.R.i.S. were very clear – it is NOT nice to turn humans into food," said the beast. "I'm surprised you don't know that already, Bethany."

"I'm not talking about humans as food," said Bethany through gritted teeth. "I'm talking about food that humans eat. Like this cheese sandwich, for instance. Would you like to try a bite?"

Bethany held the cheese sandwich out to the beast. The beast's tongues quivered on either side of its mouth.

"I probably shouldn't," said the beast nervously.

"Why not?" said Bethany. "It's only cheese. If you don't like it, you can always spit it out."

Bethany was playing a risky game, and she knew it.

The beast snaked its tongues towards the sandwich.

"Just one bite," said Bethany. "One bite isn't gonna hurt anyone."

The beast closed its eyes and wrapped its tongues around the baguette. It let some of the cheese fall on to its tongues before it took a tiny little bite.

"Oh mysies," said the beast.

The blacks of its three eyes widened and shone with glee. A rumble and a cackle emerged from the bottom of its belly – first low and gentle, then louder and so forceful that the whole hallway was filled with the stench of the beast's cabbagey breath.

"Moresies – pleeeease," said the beast, as it finished the baguette with a single gulp.

Bethany didn't know whether to scream with dread or delight. The beast was scaring her, but it also thrilled her – because she felt that this sort of behaviour would definitely be enough to convince D.o.R.R.i.S. that the beast was still a threat.

"Moresies?" said the beast.

"It's all gone," said Bethany, as she heard Ebenezer begin his descent back downstairs.

"Moresies!" said the beast, with a slight snarl.

"I-I really don't have any more. You ate the whole baguette," said Bethany.

"I said . . . MORESIES!" roared the beast. "DON'T MAKE ME ASK AGAIN, YOU FOOLISH CHILD, OR I'LL MAKE YOU SORRY!"

The Midnight Raid

"Oopsiekins," said the beast, raising a tiny hand to its mouth. Its eyes returned to normal and its voice was no longer trembling with rage. "I have no idea where that came from. Maybe I'm allergywerge to cheese sandwiches."

Bethany was furious with how quickly the beast had snapped out of its hangry rage. She had been so awed by its behaviour that she hadn't managed to push the button in time.

"Oh, don't pretend like you don't know what that was," said Bethany. "It wasn't cheese that made you like that, it was the meat hidden underneath it."

"Whaaaaat?" The beast looked genuinely horrified. "You fed me meatsies? Why ever would you do that?"

"To save the neighbourhood from whatever evil scheme you've got for it," said Bethany. "I knew a taste of meat would bring out the real you."

"But that wasn't the real me! The sandwich unleashy-weashed something . . ." The beast looked at its belly, as if unable to articulate the horrors dwelling inside it. "Unleashy-weashed something . . . nastykins."

At that moment, Ebenezer came bumbling downstairs with two armfuls of antique silver. Both piles kept wobbling from side to side, but somehow he managed not to drop any of it.

"What was that sound?" asked Ebenezer, as he laid the silver in front of the beast. "I could have sworn I heard something."

"Your ears must need a licky-wick. No noisies here!" said the beast. It let out a laugh that sounded like a goat farting, followed by a stinky fake yawn. "Oofsies. I'm awfully tiredykins. Time for beddy-byes."

"No!" shouted Bethany. "You did hear something. It was the sound of the beast revealing that it's still evil!"

"Oh, Bethany, when are you going to give this up?" asked Ebenezer in exasperation. He turned to the beast. "Don't you want to treat yourself to a nibble of all this silver I've brought you?"

"Oh nooosies," said the beast. It climbed into its canoe and wiggled its fingers. "Not hungry any more."

Bethany opened her mouth to try and tell Ebenezer again about what had happened, before realising that he would never believe her while the beast was looking so well-behaved. If she wanted to convince him of the truth, then she'd have to find a way of feeding it again.

"Yeah, well, I'm REALLY HUNGRY!" she shouted. "IN FACT I THINK I'M GOING TO MAKE MYSELF A SANDWICH USING INGREDIENTS FROM ONE OF THE REALLY MEATY FRIDGES!"

The beast paused on the staircase for a moment. Then it whooshed the canoe back up to the attic.

"A late-night sandwich, eh?" asked Ebenezer. "Mmm, that does sound rather tasty. Would you mind making me one as well?"

Bethany looked at Ebenezer, unable to believe how he was so stupid.

"Bog off and make one yourself, Ebenezer. I'm going to bed, and I'm gonna sleep down here," she said. She stomped into the front sitting room and slumped on a sofa.

"Are you quite sure, Bethany?" asked Ebenezer. "Shouldn't

you try and get the best sleep possible for this sweet-shop thingy tomorrow?"

"I'll sleep where I flipping want," said Bethany.

"Right – yes, of course," said Ebenezer. He scratched his head. "Um, well, I suppose I'll head up as well. Nighty-night!"

Bethany responded to the nighty-night by blowing a raspberry. She waited until she heard him leave, then she sat back up again.

Bethany had stayed downstairs because she was certain that the beast would make its way back down here to have its wicked way with the meat fridges. She switched off all the lights, so that the beast would think the coast was clear.

Now all she had to do was wait.

The waiting part was surprisingly tricky. The darkness was making her sleepy, and falling sleep is never more tempting than when you tell yourself that you must, UNDER NO CIRCUMSTANCES WHATSOEVER, sleep.

The day had been an exhausting one, and it weighed heavily on both her mind and her eyes. To stay awake, she reached into her back pocket and removed the picture of the moustachioed man, the moustacheless woman and her scowling baby self.

One of her favourite games was to make up histories for the parents she knew nothing about. Back in the orphanage, she had imagined her parents as pirates and cowboys; arctic explorers who hadn't returned because they were imprisoned by evil penguins; magicians whose trick had gone wrong when they'd accidentally disappeared each other out of existence. But ever since Bethany had tried being a do-gooder, she had taken to imagining her parents as exclusively good and wonderful people.

In tonight's fantasies, her parents were peacemakers stranded in the middle of some horrid war; spies thwarting villainy wherever they saw it; superheroes constantly kicking asteroids away from the planet. The game did wonders for keeping Bethany awake – so much so, that she was still playing it as the sun began to rise.

Bethany was just in the middle of imagining the moustachioed man and the moustacheless woman as a pair of firefighters, battling against the most violent volcano monsters the world had ever seen, when she heard something on the stairs.

It's strange when you hear a sound in the middle of the night. You're never quite sure whether you've heard it, until something else happens. For Bethany, the something else happening was the sight of the kitchen light being flicked on, and then quickly off again.

Bethany wanted to grab the Nickle-summoning button and sprint into the kitchen – but, with great restraint, she forced herself to creep. She wanted to make absolutely sure she was calling Nickle back with *evidence* that the beast couldn't be trusted.

From the hallway, she could see the kitchen. The main light was still off, but the room was faintly lit, partly by the rising sun and partly by the fridge light. There was also a

disgusting, slithery sort of gargling sound.

Bethany peered into the kitchen – and saw the beast munching, gobbling and crunching its way through the food in the meat fridges. The beast's back was turned, so she couldn't see how villainous it was looking.

Bethany edged slowly into the kitchen. The beast's feeding noises were louder now. She could see that its tongues were flying all over the place – snatching, crunching and gobbling up the contents of the fridge like two greedy tentacles. Every time the beast ate something meaty, it let

out a disgusting sort of mewing sound, followed by a low, cabbagey cackle.

The beast finished the contents of the first fridge and licked every inch of the insides. Still not satisfied, it curled its tongues around the sides of the fridge, ripped it from the walls, and crunched it into edible, metallic paste.

"Bleurghsies – tastes like scrap metal," said the beast. "MEAT is sooooo much tastier."

The beast waddled over to the next fridge, which was filled with meat. It let out a giggle of glee, like a toddler who's just stepped into a toy shop.

It was the perfect time to summon Mr Nickle. Bethany fished the button from her pocket, but couldn't bring herself to do it just yet. The sight of the beast nibbling, licking, crunching and tearing on everything from rib racks to toads-in-the-hole made her question why on earth she'd thought feeding her nemesis had been a good idea. Every bite seemed to make it ravenous for more.

Her hand trembled at the sight. She tried to jab the button, but because of the trembles and the darkness, she accidentally jabbed the side, which caused the button to leap out of her hand like a reckless coin toss.

The button echoed as it bounced on the floor. Bethany

reached for the trumpet down the back of her trousers, but her elbow accidentally caught a switch, which flooded the kitchen with light.

The beast snapped its head around. Its teeth were bared and its eyes wild, like a cornered rat. Its eyes suddenly softened when it saw who was in the kitchen.

"Bethany?" asked the beast. Its mouth was dribbly with red and pinkish meat juices. "What are you doing?"

Bethany couldn't think of a good answer.

"What are *you* doing?" she asked instead.

The beast closed the fridge and started waddling around the kitchen, fiddling nervously with its hands.

"You should never have introduced me to this type of food," said the beast. "The scrappy-wap never made me feel like this."

"Feel like what?" asked Bethany.

"All this meaty food . . . the more I eat, the more I want. It's like there's some pit or cavesies, right at the bottom of my belly that's hungry for more, more, MORE!" said the beast, now waddling around in a rather desperate sort of circle. "I don't know how to explain it, except to say that this pit likes the food – but it doesn't like it *enough*. It's crying out for something meatier, something more, something

". . . oh, I don't even want to say it."

"Say it," said Bethany.

"I think it wants something . . . something . . . something with a pulsies," said the beast, raising its tiny hands to its face.

Bethany tightened her grip around the trumpet. The emergency button was on the floor between her and the beast. She didn't want to step any closer to it though, because then she'd be in tongues' reach of the beast's mouth.

The beast followed Bethany's eyes and saw the button on the floor. Bethany was expecting it to react with rage and fury – but instead, it just looked devastated.

"Is that why you're here, Bethany?" it asked, sounding like there was a lump in its throats. "Is that why you fed me that sandwich? Was it all to get me back in my cage?"

Bethany didn't say anything, but the beast nodded as if it knew the answer already. It stretched out one of its tongues and picked the button off the floor.

Bethany cursed herself for being so clumsy. Now the beast had the button, there was no telling what it might do.

The beast paused for a moment. Then it tossed the button back to Bethany. She caught it with one hand, and frowned.

"I'm not evil – for realsies," said the beast. "My memmies *are* all gone, and all I want to do is become a better beast. Believe me, Bethany – pleasies."

For a moment, Bethany had her very first doubt. Then everything the beast had done to her in the past flashed back in her head – and she jabbed the button as hard as she could.

The Ultimate De-Beasting

The beast looked incredibly mournful for a moment. Then it sprang into action. As the puddle portal opened in the kitchen, it quickly used its tongues to wash its face and clear all evidence of its eating spree.

Mr Nickle popped out of the puddle, wearing a nightcap and worn-out PJs.

"What is it?" he asked in a sleepy voice.

"It's the beast! It was eating meat," said Bethany in triumph.

Mr Nickle rubbed his eyes, and looked at the beast. Bethany looked over, expecting a moment of victory, only to realise it was too late. The beast was smiling a sweet, dribbly smile, and was holding a fork in one of its tiny hands.

"Oh dearsies, I am eating – but deffy-weff not any meatsies," said the beast. It chomped the top off the fork. "This cutlery is delishy-wish!"

Bethany had nothing she could do or say to prove her word against the beast's.

Mr Nickle wrinkled his wrinkly face crossly at her and confiscated the button. "*These* are only for people who can be trusted with them," he said, as he put the button in his pyjama pocket. With that, he disappeared back inside the puddle.

Bethany was unable to believe how badly she had failed.

"Sorrykins for doing all that tidying," said the beast. "I know it was very sneaky of me, but I just couldn't bear the idea of leaving my homesies."

Bethany began to fear that the beast would never leave. If she couldn't even get it to reveal its true nature by feeding it some meat, then how long would it stay? Days . . . weeks . . . months . . . years, even? Maybe its evil scheme was to stay with Bethany for the rest of her life, and torment her until she was on her deathbed.

"Did you hear me, Bethany? Oh, I do hope you can forgive me," said the beast.

Bethany stomped out of the kitchen, towards the back of the house.

She couldn't believe that the beast had got the better of her – again. No matter what she did, no matter how hard she tried, it always seemed like the beast was going to find a way to stay in her life – eating away any hope of happiness.

She grabbed a blanket and went out to the garden. Raising a hand to her face, she was unsurprised to find that there were tears of frustration leaking out of her eyes.

She stayed out there as the sun continued to rise – watching as the day of her big party dawned. It should have felt like a moment of triumph. But, thanks to the beast, it didn't feel like a triumph at all. She was all out of ideas.

At some point, Bethany removed the trumpet from her trousers and held it in front of her leaking eyes. Up until a couple of days ago, she thought she was free from the beast, and she couldn't remember a period in her life when she'd been happier.

Bethany let out a little scream of frustration – wishing there was some

way of getting rid of the beast once and for all – when something in the sky caught her eye.

The something was purple and feathery, and it was flying towards the house with the speed and determination of an angry tornado. Within the blink of an eye, it landed in front of Bethany, shedding a shower of feathers.

Bethany could tell from the look of fury in the Wintlorian purple-breasted parrot's eyes that this was not a social visit.

"Bethany, I presume?" spat Mortimer. "I'm going to need you to point me in the direction of the beast."

The Murderous Mortimer

"You smell . . . wonderful," said Bethany. She knew she was talking like Eduardo Barnacle, but she couldn't help it – the scent filling her nostrils was delightful.

"I've been flying for hours, I smell sweaty," said Mortimer. His odour was fresh and earthy, like the playful smell of gardenias in the night air, because Wintlorians had kindly evolved the ability to secrete less odious odours from their sweat glands. "You smell . . . well, you just smell. Maybe you should think of changing your jumper some time, Bethany."

"How the flip do you know my name?" asked Bethany. "Nah, actually, scratch that – who the flip are you?"

"My name is Mortimer. And, unlike the rest of my species, I'm not much one for small talk. Take me to the beast –*now*."

"You look younger than the other parrots I've met," said Bethany. "How old are you?"

"Old enough," said Mortimer defensively.

Bethany and Mortimer exchanged a look. They recognised an anger in each other that they could understand.

"Why exactly are you here?" asked Bethany.

Mortimer clicked his tongue in his beak. "I'm going to kill the beast," he said, watching Bethany's face for a reaction. "I'm going to pluck out its eyes and tear apart its flesh with my talons. I plan on taking my time with it – and I promise I'll make sure that it receives three dollops of pain for every ounce of suffering it has caused Claudette."

Bethany didn't like to think of herself as weak or squeamish, but Mortimer's talk of eye-plucking and flesh-tearing had made her feel nauseous. It took a few moments to steel herself. She wanted to defeat the beast, and now a solution had literally just flown into her lap.

"Does Claudette know?" asked Bethany.

"Of course not," said Mortimer.

"Maybe we should call her," said Bethany.

"I doubt she'd be strong enough to answer," said Mortimer. Purple tears formed in his eyes, but he quickly blinked them away. "Stop stalling. Either help me, or step aside."

Bethany's conscience wondered what all her friends would think – Claudette, Muddle, Geoffrey, even stupid Ebenezer. She couldn't imagine that any of them would approve of the thoughts inside her head.

Her brain started rattling out reasons why she should let Mortimer do his worst.

If she hadn't met him, he might have tried to kill the beast anyway. By stepping aside and clearing the way, she wasn't actually doing anything bad *herself*. In some ways, she was actually doing *good*. Because the world would certainly be a better place without the beast.

"I'm not a parrot who likes to wait," said Mortimer.

Bethany's mind was made up. She owed it to herself to do everything she could to get rid of the beast.

"There's a man named Ebenezer in the house who might try to stop you," she said. "But we're going to a party this morning, so the beast will be by itself. That will help you."

"I don't need any help," snapped Mortimer. "Why does everyone think I need help?"

"Don't be an idiot," said Bethany. "You need all the help

you can get. The beast is pretending it's lost its mind, but don't be fooled – it could reveal its true self at any moment."

"I hope it does," said Mortimer. "That way I can see the evil in its eyes before I pluck them out."

"If it decides to make its move, we're all doomed," said Bethany. "If you wanna kill the beast, you'll have to do it fast – and you have to do it with this."

Bethany lifted the trumpet to Mortimer's face. She was reluctant to hand it over, because it was the only thing that made her feel protected, now that the button was gone.

"You've got to be kidding me," said Mortimer. "My talons are sharper than any trumpet."

"Yeah, and the beast's teeth are sharper than anything in the world," said Bethany. "Go with the trumpet – trust me."

Bethany's conscience started getting noisy again. "Let me get Ebenezer out of the house. Stay here until you hear me slam the front door. I'll make sure you hear it."

Mortimer grunted in begrudging agreement.

Bethany walked quickly back inside, shoving her fingers in her ears to try and block out the conscience. She only removed them when she was next to the kitchen door.

"No, no, bestie – I'm putting my foot downsies," she

heard the beast say to Ebenezer. "There, do you see how downsies it is? I am not coming to the sweet shop. It's Bethany's big day, and I'm not going to spoil it for her. I know she still doesn't like meesies."

It seemed Bethany wouldn't have to persuade the beast to stay after all. She glanced back towards the garden, and suddenly wondered whether she was doing the right thing.

"Well, I think that's rotten of you," said Ebenezer. "I was so looking forward to you vomiting out some more things for the neighbourhood."

Bethany took a few deep breaths, and walked into the kitchen in as relaxed a fashion as she could manage.

"Come on, Ebenezer, time for us to go," said Bethany. She made a point of looking at the clock, even though her eyes were too blurry to see the numbers. "We'll be the last to arrive if we leave it any longer."

Bethany could see Ebenezer hesitating. She had to get him out of the house.

"Don't you want to hear what all the people at the sweet shop think about your do-gooding?" she asked.

Ebenezer bit his lip. Bethany knew how much he adored the praise of strangers.

"Oh, dash it," said Ebenezer. He turned to the beast. "Final chance. Are you sure you don't want to come?"

"I don't want the beast at my party," said Bethany. "It has to stay here."

"I've already done enough to spoil Bethany's lifesies," said the beast. "I won't ruin her party as well."

"Yeah," said Bethany. Her voice wobbled.

Ebenezer headed for the door. Bethany went to follow him, but the beast called her back.

"Oh, and one more thing," it said. "Sorrykins for making you feel poopy. I don't know how yet, but I prommy-wom that I will find a way for us to be friendsies."

The beast smiled a weak, dribbly smile. Bethany turned her back and followed Ebenezer out of the house. She paused before slamming the front door, knowing that this would be all the signal Mortimer needed.

"Ready?" asked Ebenezer, as he climbed into the driving seat of the car.

"Yeah . . . yeah, I am," she answered. She slammed the door as hard as she could, and joined Ebenezer in the car.

The Beast and the Parrot

The beast wondered why Bethany had slammed the door so loudly. It hoped that it hadn't done anything to put her in a bad mood. Then, with a great effort of will, it slowly climbed to its feet.

It was determined to find a way to befriend Bethany. It chewed its tongues thoughtfully, and wondered about preparing a few ickle surprises for when they came back from the party.

The beast was just thinking about what marvellous things it could vomit out for her, when its belly started rumbling and grumbling again. The sound was becoming more regular and ravenous, ever since the beast had eaten the meaty sandwich.

"Shh, shh, shushykins!" the beast said to its belly. "You're not getting what you want so stop asking for it. You're just going to have to stop thinking of humany food."

This was easier said than done. Every time the beast tried to think of something other than food, the belly would make an unpleasant, angry sort of noise, which would get the beast thinking all over again about poultry and piggies, ribs and roast beef, fat juicy chicken legs, and tiny little bones it could snap so easily with its lovely, lovely –

"MUST STOP THINKING ABOUT FOOD," said the beast, slapping its belly with its tongues.

The belly responded by growling even angrier, and the beast in return responded by slapping it even harder. The rumbling combined with the slapping was like some sinister bongo drum.

The beast took a deep breath. As it breathed in, it detected a new scent in the air. The smell was inside the house. It was fresh and earthy, and it smelled . . . absolutely *delicious*.

The new smell was quickly joined by the arrival of a new noise – a strange, stifled sort of squawk, which sounded like it was coming from inside the house. At first, the beast thought it must have misheard, but then there was another squawk.

"Hellosies?" said the beast. "I say, HELLOSIES?!"

The beast was greeted with so much silence that it began to doubt whether it had heard anything at all. It used its tongues to clear out its ears – but while the earwax was sizzling on its tongues, it heard something else. It heard something which sounded awfully like the flapping of wings.

A few seconds later, a young male Wintlorian purple-breasted parrot flew into the room, carrying a trumpet in his talons.

"There's no one to protect you now, is there?" said the parrot, with a beaky smirk. "Get ready to say hello to the talons of Mortimer!"

The Soured Sweet Shop

As Ebenezer beeped and honked the car over to the sweet shop, Bethany's conscience grew noisier and noisier. The closer they got to the party, the more she felt that she didn't have any right to be there.

"When are you going to stop being annoyed with me?" asked Ebenezer.

"You what?" said Bethany.

"About the beast," said Ebenezer. "You keep calling me Ebenezer, instead of gitface – it doesn't feel right."

"I thought you hated being called gitface," said Bethany.

"I did. But now that you haven't said it for a few days, I kind of miss it," said Ebenezer. "And I want to know what

I can do to earn my nickname back."

Bethany's noisy conscience wasn't getting any quieter with Ebenezer being nice to her. Normally, she didn't like discussing her problems, because she somehow felt that it made them more real, but on this occasion she decided that a conversation was preferable to being left alone with her guilty thoughts.

"I hate the beast," she said bluntly. "I hate it more than anyone else in the world. And I hate you and everyone else who thinks the creature who ate me alive – TWICE! – could possibly be capable of change. So right now, there's no flipping way I'm going to call you gitface ever again."

Ebenezer parked the car on the next street – the last free space. It seemed as if pretty much the whole neighbourhood was visiting the sweet shop. He didn't say anything until they were out of the car, and walking on the street.

"I know I did bad by taking the beast around the neighbourhood without asking you first," said Ebenezer. "And I suppose . . . if I think about it . . . I've sort of been doing double bad by taking credit for all the beast's gifts. But I was inspired to do it, because of you."

"You what?" said Bethany.

"Let's face it, Bethany. You're much better than me

at do-gooding – it just seems to come easier to you," said Ebenezer. "I suppose I might have been taking some credit for the beast's work, because I was jealous . . . because I wanted to feel what it was like to be successful at do-gooding like you."

Bethany opened her mouth to tell Ebenezer that she really wasn't as good at do-gooding as he thought, but he wasn't quite finished.

"Before we met, I was a selfish git who cared about nothing and no one but myself and my pretty clothes," said Ebenezer. "While you . . . well, your idea of a good afternoon was to shove worms up poor Geoffrey's nostrils. But since we've teamed up to try and be better sort of people, I think we've changed. And if you can inspire me to change five centuries' worth of bad habits, then there's no reason why the beast can't change as well."

"The beast will NEVER change," said Bethany.

"I think it has," said Ebenezer. "Admittedly that's mainly due to the whole memory-loss thingy, but –"

"Nah. Don't say that," said Bethany. "The beast doesn't deserve a second chance."

"I don't think I really deserved much of a second chance either, but your friendship gave me one," said Ebenezer.

"And I know it'll take a while. But when you see all the wonderful things we can do with a good beast in the world – I think you'll change your mind."

They had made it to the sweet shop. Ebenezer stepped inside, but Bethany lingered for a moment by the doors. She looked back towards the fifteen-storey house, thinking about what was probably going on in the fifteen-storey house at that exact moment.

It wasn't a good feeling.

The Return of the Beast

"What's a Mortimer?" asked the beast, as it looked behind the strange, purple-feathered visitor. "Is the Mortimer coming soonykins?"

"Mortimer's here already," said the parrot, his eyes ablaze. "And soon Mortimer will happen to you."

"Mortimers sound like most exciting thingsies!" said the beast.

"I am Mortimer!" said Mortimer. He stretched his wings to their fullest span, and tightened his grip around the trumpet. "And I am NOT exciting. I'm horrider than you can ever imagine."

The beast scratched its blobby head. "I was just thinking

how adorable you looked. The gold of the shiny thingy goes well with the purple."

"I am not adorable. I'm abominable!" said Mortimer.

"Oh dearsies. Sorrykins for the confusion," said the beast. "I'm sure you're scary to lots of people."

"I don't want you to be sorry, I want to *make* you sorry," snapped Mortimer. He dangled the trumpet menacingly in his talons. "And I'm going to do it with this."

The beast smiled at the parrot. It wasn't sure what the bird was on about, but it was all very entertaining.

"I said, I'm going to do it . . . with THIS!" said Mortimer, dangling the trumpet even closer to the beast. The beast just smiled again. "Doesn't it terrify you?"

"Not particularly," said the beast. "Lots of people carry them around me. I've never been exactly sure why, but I felt too shy to ask. I can do pretendsies if you like, though?"

Mortimer squawked with frustration and threw the trumpet across the room.

"I knew Bethany was joking!" he growled.

"Ooh, do you know Bethany? How exciting!" said the beast. "I'm afraid she just left."

"I know she left. She left you to me," snarled Mortimer. "In fact, she's the one who cleared the path for your DEATH."

The beast laughed nervously. It backed away from Mortimer, stumbling over a chair.

"You must be thinking of a different Bethany," it said.

"Scowly face, snotty nose, smelly jumper? No, I've got the right one," said Mortimer. He hovered over the beast as it waddled backwards. "She hates you. I think she might hate you even more than me. The two of us – we planned this together."

"Wh-what did you plansies?" asked the beast.

Mortimer dragged his talons together.

"Watch out," said the beast. "You could poke out someone's eyesies with those."

"Oh, I know," said Mortimer. "I think we'll start with the middle one."

The beast couldn't escape the truth any longer. There was a look of death in the parrot's eyes, and that deathly gaze was targeted firmly at the beast.

"Wh-why?" asked the beast. It continued to waddle backwards, while Mortimer flew above.

"Why? WHY?!" said Mortimer. "Because you're a monster. You're the devil in blob form who deserves a long, slow, punishing death."

"But I've changed!" said the beast. It tripped over itself

and fell to its back – unable to do anything now but watch as Mortimer circled it like a crow around a carcass. "All I want to do is make friends with Bethany and Ebby-kneesies, and spend the rest of my days doing kind and do-gooding things with them."

"Was it kind what you did to Claudette?" spat Mortimer. "Is that your idea of a *do-gooding* thing?"

The beast blinked in confusion. If it really was destined to die at the talons of an angry parrot, then it at least wanted to understand why.

"Claudette?" it asked. "I'm terribly sorrykins – that's another of those words that I just don't know."

"Don't try that with me," said Mortimer.

The beast scrunched its three eyes shut, and tried desperately to remember this 'Claudette' word. "It feels familiar to these ears," it panted. "And it rolls easily off the tongues."

"Yes, yes – remember, beast!" said Mortimer. "Let Claudette be the last thing you think about in this life!"

"Is a Claudette . . . I don't know why I'm thinking this . . . some sort of chewy, delishy-wish snack?" asked the beast.

It opened its eyes hopefully and looked up at Mortimer.

The parrot let out a furious screech.

"Oh dearsies," said the beast.

Mortimer dived, still screeching – aiming its kitchen-knife talons at the beast's middle eye, like a dart about to plunge into the bullseye.

The beast knew it was about to die.

Its actions now were pure, thoughtless instinct. Its mouth spread wider than the beast could have ever thought possible. Then, just as quickly and instinctively, the mouth snapped shut again – snapping off Mortimer's lovely sharp talons.

Mortimer gave a scream that to any normal ears would have been bloodcurdling. But, to the beast's ears, the screech sounded strangely familiar. As the beast chewed the crunchy spikes, other things started to return to its mind as well.

Agent Louie had once told Mortimer that the mind of the beast was usually dark, dangerous and prickly – like a hedgehog waiting in the shadows with a torpedo.

And now, that mind was coming back.

The Poisoned Praise

"Come on," said Ebenezer. "Let's forget about the beast for today. It's your special moment."

Bethany followed Ebenezer inside the sweet shop which was already bustling with guests. There were marshmallow mountains and candy-cane canyons, chandeliers made of frosted chocolate and walls covered with delicious treats that you could snap off with your hands. There were self-cleaning lollipop slides designed to be ridden tongue first, fondues oozing with fizzypop candy, and pick 'n' mix trolleys where even the trolleys themselves were edible.

It was all as charming as it was enchanting. But for Bethany, the pleasures were soured by the knowledge of how she had set the beast up for an execution.

"Oh no, that's not the sort of face I wanted to see, Bethany," said Miss Muddle. "It's the marshmallow mountains, isn't it? I knew they were too much. Stupid Muddle, stupid Muddle! I so wanted everything to be perfect for you, especially as I ruined the surprise part of your party!"

If Bethany's insides hadn't been squirming with guilt, she would have said something complimentary about the marshmallow mountains. She remained silent though, so Miss Muddle ran over and demolished the marshmallow mountains while some children from the orphanage were enjoying them.

As Bethany walked through the shop, she realised the sheer scale of the bad thing she had done. Her guilt wasn't helped by the fact that every person she and Ebenezer bumped into seemed to be filled with praise for the beast.

"Honestly, Mr Tweezer, you'll have to come and bleedin' see it," said the bird-keeper, who had brought along Keith the dove. "The hoatzin and the tutting ducks have become thick as thieves – and those fellas can be awfully snobby."

"Thank you so much for introducing us to your lovely dog," said the kindly old lady. "My grandaughter called from Australia today. She was so happy with her card, and there's

no way I would have been able to get it to her in time, if it hadn't been for this marvellous post box. I love it so much that I've decided to bring it as my date for the party."

"Those bandages your dog coughed out? Absolutely marvellous," said Dr Barnacle, Eduardo's equally well-nostrilled mother. "Was its name 'the Beast'? Well, it deserves a very big treat indeed. I've never known any material able to snap broken bones back together so quickly. I'm wearing one of them myself, for a wrist sprain I got the other week."

"BOOWWPPP BOOOOOWWWFIDDDDY

BOOOP!" trumpeted the lizard lady, speaking a language that could only be understood by elephants. She took off the scarf that the beast had vomited out and her voice returned to its usual croak. "Speaking with the animals in the zoo . . . it's been the happiest experience of my whole life."

Ebenezer was having a splendid time and, through a great effort of will, he made sure to give the beast extra credit for all its vomity brilliance. He wanted to know what it was like to be an actual do-gooder, and he thought being less of a credit-hog might help.

Bethany was not having such a splendid time. Hearing all the beast's actions laid out like this made her wonder whether she should have believed Ebenezer all along.

She tried to take herself away from the crowd. But everywhere she looked, she saw some banner or balloon saying 'WELL DONE, BETHANY!' or 'CONGRATULATIONS TO BETHANY – ONE OF THE BEST PEOPLE IN THE WORLD!' The praise seemed to be shaming her.

Eventually, Bethany could take it no more. She had to confess the truth.

"Oh, ah – hullo, Bethany!" said Geoffrey, just as she was gearing herself up to tell Ebenezer. He was wearing his best suit, which was about two and a half sizes too small for him. "I'm so very happy to see you, because I've got something very important that I've been trying to ask –"

"Not now, Geoffrey," said Bethany, barely even looking at him. "I'll find you later."

She grabbed hold of Ebenezer's sleeve and led him away from the crowds.

"What is it?" he asked. "I think Nurse Mindy was just about to compliment me on my lovely waistcoat."

"Soz – but this is no time for waistcoats," said Bethany. "I did something. Something really, really bad."

The Cry of Claudette

Claudette woke up with a screech that roused the whole forest of Wintloria. There was still some part of her connected to the beast.

"*Morty, noooo!*" she cried in her raspy voice. Then, in an even more terrified voice, she added, "*The beast is coming back!*"

Her distress brought Agents Hughie, Louie and Stewie to her tree – along with every other purple-breasted parrot in the forest. Her wings were quivering, and her eyes were dilating from furious black to splendid purple.

"*It's eating something with a pulse. Its personality has been trapped in a cavern of its belly, but now it's all coming back . . . every diabolical dream, pernicious pondering and mortifying* memory . . . *everything's swarming like a tornado into the beast's blobby head.*" She spoke with an intense urgency that frightened the other parrots. "*Who fed the beast? I told you all not to let it eat! I told you not to let it escape!*"

"She's delirious again," said Agent Hughie.

"Only explanation for it," said Agent Louie.

"We should up her medicine and put her back to sleep," hissed Agent Stewie.

The three of them made their way over to the D.o.R.R.i.S. beeping machine. Claudette yanked the wire out of her body and squawked at them.

"*Don't you see? The beast's whole life is flashing before its eyes, as if it's about to die . . . but really, it's being reborn. It's reliving the past few months of its life through three whole new eyes, and it doesn't like what it sees . . . It can't believe that it's been tricked into being a do-gooder. It feels angry, humiliated and . . . oh no, oh no, oh no . . . VENGEFUL!*"

"We'll find the right melody to make all your nightmares disappear," said Giuletta.

"*This is no nightmare. This is happening right now – on the other side of the world. And I have to get there . . . I have to SAVE BETHANY! She's one of my best friends.*"

"Absolutely not," said Agent Hughie.

"You can't go chasing after fantasies," said Agent Louie.

"And even if you could, the journey would kill you," hissed Agent Stewie.

Claudette knew that she wouldn't be able to live with herself if she didn't help Bethany. She spotted the high-tech device that looked awfully like an umbrella, which Agent Stewie had used to puddle port her over to Wintloria in the first place.

"Lie back down," said Giulietta. "You know you're too weak to fly."

The exertion was digging into Claudette's bones. But she readied her wings – knowing and praying that somewhere, deep down, there was the strength she needed.

"Claudette?" began Agent Hughie. "What are you –?"

With another screech, Claudette flapped her weak wings and grabbed the umbrella with her talons. She crashed several times on her way out of the tree, flapping away as quickly as she could. As she fiddled with the handle of the umbrella, she managed to open a puddle a few metres in front of her. Then she screwed her eyes shut and focused on where she wanted to arrive.

"*MUST . . . SAVE . . . BETHANY!*" she cried, as she disappeared.

The Gifts That Wouldn't Stop Giving

"You did what?!" whispered Ebenezer.

They were standing in the corner of the sweet shop, next to the basket containing the latest version of the bombastic bubbletrumpets.

Everyone else was crowding around Miss Muddle – calling for her to make a 'SPEECH! SPEECH!' The bird-keeper and Keith the dove worked together to clear a table of a leaning tower of bonbons, while Timothy and Paulo the postman helped the sweet-maker climb up.

"Um . . . oh, bother. I'm a much better sweet-maker than I am a speechmaker," said Miss Muddle. She nervously hiccupped. "But I suppose I should say a word or two about our not-so-surprised guest of honour, and the reason why we're all here . . ."

"It's terrible, I know," Bethany whispered back at Ebenezer. "I was stupid and thoughtless, and –"

"Shh!" said Eduardo Barnacle, at the back of the crowd. He flared his nostrils at them. "It's very *childish* to talk during someone's speech. Especially when that speech is about you."

". . . Um, er, I know many of you probably weren't Bethany's biggest fans when you first met her. The first time she visited this shop, she left some surprise frogs in my liquorice jars," continued Miss Muddle. "But it doesn't matter what people were like in the past. It only matters what people are like today. And today, Bethany is a very, very good . . ."

"I know it was wrong of me, Ebenezer," continued Bethany, at an even quieter volume. "But this angry parrot showed up for revenge, and I wanted to get the dribbly stinker out of our lives . . . and it just seemed like the perfect opportunity."

"To kill the beast?!" said Ebenezer. "I can't believe I wanted to be more like you!"

In his fury, he forgot to keep his voice at a whisper. Eduardo Barnacle turned around again, but not to shush them this time.

"Kill . . . the beast?" he asked in his nasally voice. "You can't kill the lovely doggy who's done such wonders for my garden!"

Before the beast had vomited out the hearing aids, the showgirl who could still do the splits at the age of eighty-nine wouldn't have heard a word of this conversation. But now she and all the other retirement-home residents caught the words with crystal clarity.

"Kill the beast?" said the showgirl. "You can't do that!"

One by one, word about the beast's potential murder spread among the crowd – until soon, each and every bird and person turned their backs on Miss Muddle so they could look at Bethany instead. Keith the dove looked particularly appalled.

"Sorry, am I boring you?" asked Miss Muddle, as she climbed down from the table. "I did tell you I'm not very good at speeches."

"Explain yourself at once!" croaked the lizard lady. "What's all this talk of killing the beast?"

"Ask her!" said Ebenezer, pointing at Bethany as if she was a great wallop of dog poop on a spotless pavement.

The crowd gathered around Bethany in a mob now.

Some started heckling her with insults. Others claimed that they always knew that Bethany was a do-badder who didn't deserve a party all along. The rest bemoaned such cruelty to a creature as kind and wonderful as the beast.

"Oh, ah – bother, please stop," shouted a voice. Everyone turned around and saw that Geoffrey had climbed on the table. "Let's allow Bethany to explain herself. She's my best . . . well, my best person, and I'm sure she wouldn't dream of doing anything like this. We wouldn't be friends if I thought she was in any way a killer. Go on, Bethany. Tell everyone that you didn't do anything to the beast."

Geoffrey smiled encouragingly at Bethany, but she couldn't even meet his eyes. Guilt was pouring out of every pore of her body. And with a single look, everyone in the room could see that she had no way of defending herself.

"Oh, Bethany, no," said Geoffrey.

Without even Ebenezer or Geoffrey by her side, Bethany had never felt more alone.

The retirement-home residents' hearing aids suddenly started to make strange noises.

"Shut up with that bleedin' racket!" shouted the bird-keeper, as Keith the dove covered his ears with his wings. "It's doin' my head in!"

"We can't!" said the showgirl. She and several other residents tried to switch the hearing aids off. "They're making a strange sort of crackling sound."

"I don't think it's a crackling," said Eduardo Barnacle, as he held his ear to one of the aids. "It sounds more like a *cackling*. And quite a sinister, slithery one at that."

Everyone listened for themselves. The sinister, slithery cackling grew louder.

"What the duck-quack?!" asked the bird-keeper, speaking for everyone in the room.

Several other objects started misbehaving as well. The spider-tidiers pushed over the displays that they had so lovingly made. The kindly old lady's post box started spitting out hate mail, addressed to every person in the sweet shop. The scarf wrapped itself tighter and tighter around the lizard lady's neck, until it made her croak for mercy. The bandages around Dr Barnacle's wrist ceased to heal, and started to break her arm in new places. The sweet shop was thrown into chaos.

Bethany and Ebenezer had seen something like this happen before. If the beast's vomit was misbehaving, that meant . . .

"The beast must still be alive," said Ebenezer. He felt

relieved, only to feel significantly less relieved a moment later.

"It's not just alive . . ." said Bethany, as she looked around at the familiar scenes of destruction. "I think it's got its flipping mind back."

The two of them looked outside. In the distance, they could see a sturdy canoe hurtling towards the sweet shop. It was travelling so fast that speed cameras were flashing all over the place, like paparazzi at a red-carpet event.

As the canoe came closer, Bethany could see the unconscious Mortimer in the back seat, surrounded by an assortment of vomit.

The gardening gnomes were stomping on either side of the canoe. They were two metres taller than they had been in Eduardo Barnacle's garden, so they were now like giants. The stink-box – still containing the poor, terrified hoatzin – was being forced to fly at a pace even faster than a bullet eagle. All the toys from the orphanage had been cannibalised into things more sinister than playful: the shape-changing Frisbees looked like pointy axes now, and the self-skipping ropes had stiffened into spears.

And riding in the midst of it all was the beast.

Bethany realised something. This was the real beast. And it was completely unlike the creature they had been

dealing with over the course of the past two days. She and Ebenezer watched as the canoe came closer and closer to the sweet shop – wondering when it was going to stop. Then they realised that the beast had absolutely no intention of stopping it at all.

Bethany pushed everyone away from the window. Ebenezer did the same with the people who were close to him

"GET BACK!" they shouted. "GET BACK, GET BACK, GET B–!"

There was an almighty shattering of glass as the canoe and the other beastly items shattered the sweet-shop windows to smithereens. Miss Muddle yelped as she saw all her work destroyed. Ebenezer scrambled in his pocket for the D.o.R.R.i.S. button – but realised it was missing.

"Sozza," said Bethany. "I nicked it off you, and Nickle nicked it off me."

The beast stood up among the wreckage, holding the train conductor's megaphone. A grin of dribble stretched across its face.

"Hello, everyone," said the beast. Its voice was positively quivering with slither. "I hope you don't mind me crashing the party-warty."

The Party Pooper

"Party! Not party-warty – PARTY!" roared the beast, severely disappointed to have its entrance spoiled by such a stupid slip of the tongues. "I do hope you don't mind me crashing the PARTY."

The beast cast its eyes around the room. The neighbours were clearly unsettled by the explosive entrance, but they weren't looking at the beast with quite the same level of horrified fear that it had grown to expect. In fact, the beast could have sworn there were looks of concern in their eyes.

It realised it was still wearing the stupid dog costume.

It pulled down the hood and wiggled its fingers to shred it to pieces.

"Are you all right, beast?" asked a small, warbly voice, belonging to the kindly old lady. "Have you just given yourself a shave?"

"All right isn't the word!" boomed the beast into its megaphone. It raised its free tiny hand triumphantly into the air. "I am majestic! I am splendid! I am the most extraordinary being to ever set foot on this pathetic little earthy-werthy! EARTH, I MEAN EARTH!"

"That is the most *splendiferous* of news," said Eduardo – thrilled to have an opportunity to use the word he had learned from that day's loo paper.

"Bethany was sayin' summat about having killed you," said the bird-keeper. "And we were so worried. It must have been another of her jokes no one gets. She used to think it funny to swap my bird feed with farting candy – strange kid."

The bird-keeper and some of the others in the room frowned at Bethany, hardly able to believe that she was capable of joking about something as unfunny as the death of the beast. However, Geoffrey beamed with delight. The 'joke' explanation made perfect sense to him.

"Have you come to help us, beast?" asked Dr Barnacle,

wincing with pain from the arm-breaking bandages. "I think some of your presents are a little out of control."

"*Please, lovely beast . . .*" croaked the lizard lady, as she battled with the scarf, ". . . *help us.*"

Bethany crawled towards a fallen tower of Miss Muddle's sweets, grabbed two creations and shoved one at Ebenezer.

"Help you?" spat the beast. "I am not here to *help* you. I was the one who got the vomit to misbehave in the first place, you idiots!"

Some of the neighbours frowned. Others laughed.

"Why are you all looking at me like this?" asked the beast, with a snarly slither. "Have you no sense? Do you have no idea of who I am?"

"Course we know – silly ickle beasty," said Amy Clue – a bear-carrying toddler from the orphanage. "You's a kind and speshul friend. Nuffin' scary 'bout beasty."

The toddler's voice was little, but her words were greeted with gusto by the rest of the neighbours. None of them seemed to be afraid. The beast didn't like it one little bit, because it didn't know how it was supposed to respond.

"Nothing scary, eh?" said the beast. "Nothing scary about . . . THIS?!"

The beast wiggled its fingers and set its vomit to work.

The giant gnomes bent down and shone their red eyes into the neighbours' faces. The hoatzin's stink-box amplified the bird's odours so the whole shop was filled with a sickening scent. The axe-shaped Frisbees started flying around the room – making everyone duck, out of fear of decapitation.

"This is me – ALL ME!" said the beast, its eyes blazing with fury. "I'm the one who's doing this! Think I'm kind? Think I'm *speshul* now?"

The atmosphere in the room changed immediately. The familiar sound of ear-piercing screams and wide-eyed looks of sheer fear were all on display.

The beast smiled, preparing to relish the moment. But, for some reason, the sights and sounds didn't bring any joy to its dark soul. There was even a voice in the back of its head saying that what it was doing was 'totally-wotally wrongsies'.

The beast looked around the sweet shop for a distraction. It found Bethany and Ebenezer.

"Actually – it's not ALL me," the beast roared into its megaphone. "How can I possibly take credit for all this when there are two such very important people to thank? If you're feeling afraid for your life right about now, then know that there are two people who deserve your fears as well . . . Bethany and Ebenezer!"

"I'm sorry, Bethany," said Ebenezer, as he ducked from an axe-Frisbee. "The beast isn't capable of change. I should have just left it locked up in its cage and had nothing to do with it."

"Nah – I'm the one to blame," said Bethany. "If I hadn't meddled, the real beast might've never come back."

Neither of them were huggers – even in a life or death situation – so they had developed their own alternative. Bethany bent her head, while Ebenezer gave it a pat.

"You see?" the beast spat into the megaphone. "They've as good as confessed. THEY are the ones responsible for what is happening to you right now! If Ebenezer hadn't tricked me into vomiting all these gifty-wifts, then I wouldn't be using them to attack you. And if Bethany hadn't spoiled my life by freeing my mind, then I would still be the good, kind beast you all thought you knew!"

Bethany knew she should be screaming just about now. But there was something in the beast's words that gave her cause for puzzlement.

"Spoiled?" she said.

"Eh?" said the beast.

"Spoiled . . . you just said she spoiled your life," said

235

Ebenezer. "Don't you like having your mind back?"

"Of course I do! My mind is wonderful and cunning! My mind is me – and me is the beesies' little kneesie-weesies!" said the beast. It slapped itself across the face for all the STUPIDY-WUPIDY baby talk.

At this moment, a puddle burst into the sweet shop. It was a deeply unstable puddle – opening first in the ruins of the marshmallow mountains, then in several places on the lickable slide, before reappearing on the treat-covered walls.

It eventually settled on the ceiling, but started sparking and groaning instead of fizzing and hissing. A moment later, Claudette tumbled out of it, bringing down one of the frozen chocolate chandeliers as she did so. The puddle promptly disappeared.

"Claudette?" asked Bethany. For a moment she was ecstatic with joy, before immediately growing itchy with fear for her beloved friend. "You shouldn't be here! Get back!"

But it was too late. The high-tech umbrella had snapped in Claudette's talons as she fell to the ground.

The journey had not been kind to the parrot. One of her wings was bent, her beak was dented, and she was shedding feathers as if the colour purple was going out of fashion.

"Hello, poppet," said Claudette. Her voice was even

weaker than before, and every word seemed like a struggle. *"I've come . . . to save you."*

The sight of Claudette so weak brought tears to Bethany's eyes, and lumps to Ebenezer's throat. However, the person in the room who seemed most affected was the beast.

The beast had never been squeamish around anything. In fact, horrifying sights generally made it either cackle or lick its lips. And yet, for some reason, it was having difficulty looking at Claudette.

"Did I . . . did I do this to you?" asked the beast.

Claudette barely had any energy left to speak, let alone fly. And yet still, with her bent wings and her dented beak, she was determined to save Bethany. She hobbled towards the beast.

"What are you doing?" asked the beast.

"*Must . . . stop . . . beast,*" said Claudette, wincing with pain. "*Must . . . save . . . Bethany!*"

"You think you can stop me? There's not a single person in this whole sweet shop who can stop me!" said the beast.

It opened its mouth to let out a triumphant cackle, but nothing happened.

"*I've felt your mind. I know that it . . . was different,*" said Claudette, as she hobbled closer to the beast. "*You must have those memories too. They must . . . have had an effect. Maybe the right song . . . or word . . . or . . .*"

"It's no use. That pathetic version of me died when I munched the talons off your friend. You've lost. When I look at you, there's only one thing I feel," said the beast. It tried to make itself enjoy the spectacle of Claudette's suffering – just like it had enjoyed the suffering of so many others in the past. "What I feel is . . . SORRYKINS!"

The Enthusiastic Victim

"Not sorrykins! Sensational! I meant to say sensational," said the beast, slapping itself again. "Slip of the tongues," it said pompously. "Just a little slip of the tongues."

"That seems to be happening loads," said Bethany, scowling at the beast. "You're talking like . . . like you were before your mind came back."

"NO, I'M NOT!" said the beast, stamping one of its tiny feet. "I haven't changed at all! So you can get that stupid idea out of your snot-filled head!"

"Who said anything about being changed?" said Bethany.

"*We* didn't bring it up," said Ebenezer. "Have you *changed*, beast?"

"ABSOLUTELY NOT!" roared the beast. "Does it look like I've changed to you?"

The beast motioned at the chaos and screams in the room. It was enraged when Bethany, Ebenezer and Claudette did actually have a look – and took their time doing it.

"You let the lizard lady go," said Bethany. "While you were talking to us, the scarf slithered off her neck."

The lizard lady was croaking and panting for breath. "*My name . . . is . . . Barbara,*" she croaked. Unfortunately, her croak was too quiet for anyone to hear.

"That was an accident!" said the beast. It wiggled its fingers at the scarf. The scarf started wrapping itself around the lizard lady's neck again – until the beast wiggled its fingers once more and let the scarf fall limply to the floor. "And I don't have to prove myself to you!"

"You haven't decapitated anyone yet," said Ebenezer, as he looked around at all the screaming yet full-headed neighbours in the room. "In fact – I don't think the Frisbees are low enough to give people so much as a haircut."

Lying at the bottom of the canoe in the middle of the sweet shop, Mortimer groaned and stirred. For the first time, Bethany, Ebenezer and Claudette noticed the bandages around the parrot's talons and the ropes tying it up.

"*Morty's . . . alive?*" rasped Claudette with joy.

"Why didn't you eat him?" asked Bethany. "It must have been a right pain tying him up. And those bandages look like the ones you vomited out for Dr Barnacle. Did you heal Mortimer?"

"His blood was making a mess on my pretty kitchen floor," said the beast. "And if you must know, I didn't eat him because I was saving my appetite."

Ebenezer laughed at this. The beast treated him to a three-eyed glare that could have frightened the skin off a badger, but Ebenezer didn't stop.

"You never save your appetite," said Ebenezer, still chuckling. "You *have* changed!"

"I have NOT changed!" roared the beast. "I'll drink the insides out of that parrot's talons like a sippy cup! I'll wiggle my fingers and chop off the heads of every stupid neighbour here, if you want me to."

"No!" pleaded Claudette.

Ebenezer got to his knees. "Oh, please, beast. Don't do it!"

The beast smiled. Finally, it was getting the respect it deserved.

"Go on then," said Bethany.

The beast snapped its head at the brat.

"What did you say, snot-brain?" asked the beast.

"I said, go on then," said Bethany. She had told enough fibs in her life to be able to spot a liar. "I don't think you have it in you any more. Prove. Me. Wrong."

"I am the builder and destroyer of empires!" spat the beast. "I have done things that would make your puny brain leak out of your ears, and I have vomited cruelty that would cause your jaw to fall to your ankles! I am –"

"Yeah, yeah – terrifying, powerful, we get it," said Bethany, rolling her eyes. "Stop threatening to do evil, and just flipping get on with it. If you've got it in you, that is."

"FINE!" said the beast. "But remember – you asked for this . . ."

The beast chucked the megaphone into its belly. It stretched out both of its tiny hands, preparing to decapitate an entire neighbourhood by wiggling its fingers like it had never wiggled them before.

"Here we go . . ." said the beast.

Bethany pretended to yawn. She watched as the beast willed its fingers to wiggle – first it stared at one hand, and then the other. Beads of sweat started leaking from every inch of its flesh. Every time it tried to wiggle, nothing happened.

Finally, the beast dropped its tiny hands to its sides. Bethany grinned. She was right.

The beast's eyes suddenly gleamed.

"I can't do it because I'm waiting to kill *you*, Bethany," said the beast, relieved to have found an explanation for its behaviour. "I've been waiting for so long to eat you, and I simply won't be able to kill or chew upon anyone else until you're in my belly. Oh, Bethany, Bethany – when I get my fangs on you –"

Bethany took a step forward.

"Go on then," she said – again. "Do. It."

"Oh, I would. Believe you me, I *WOULD*," said the beast. "You're just lucky you're holding that trumpet."

Bethany had forgotten about the bombastic bubbletrumpet she had picked up from the floor as a weapon. She glanced at Ebenezer. He was still holding his bubbletrumpet as well.

Bethany thought for a moment. Her gambles were getting bigger and bigger – and this next one would literally be a matter of life and death. But, for some reason, she was feeling confident.

"What? This trumpet?" asked Bethany. She raised the bombastic bubbletrumpet to her mouth and took a big, fat bite. Then she tossed it behind her. "I don't think you're gonna be able to use that as an excuse, do you?"

She took another step towards the beast. She was now close enough to slap its face.

"How long have you been waiting for a chance like this?" she asked. She didn't miss the opportunity to slap the beast, and gave it a nice big thwack – right on its blobby flesh. "This is what you've wanted all along, isn't it? Come on, beast. EAT ME."

The Battle Inside
the Beast

"Don't do it, Bethany!" cried Claudette. She started wobbling on her talons because she was so exhausted.

"Get back – NOW!" shouted Ebenezer. He tried to pull Bethany back from the beast, but she pushed him away.

"Oh, ah – bother, bother. Please don't eat Bethany," said Geoffrey. He ran forward, tripping over some spilled marmalicious gobblecracks. "Eat me instead."

"Nah – that's not gonna work. There's only one child the beast wants," said Bethany. She was holding her hands tight behind her back now, because she didn't want the beast to see that they were trembling. "What do you say, beast? You feeling peckish?"

Everyone in the sweet shop was watching. The beast felt the eyes on its skin, and it didn't care for the pressure. It's awfully hard not to feel self-conscious when everyone's watching you eat.

The beast came up with a simple solution to its stage fright. It wiggled its fingers at the hoatzin stink-box, and got it to emit a gas that knocked out everyone in the room except itself, Bethany and Ebenezer. It wanted Ebenezer to watch Bethany's death, as punishment for all the do-gooding he had tricked the beast into doing.

"Any last words?" asked the beast.

"Yeah – four," said Bethany. She could feel her legs start to wobble. Fortunately, the beast hadn't noticed. "Get. On. With. It."

Bethany scrunched her eyes shut. So did the beast. It was hard to tell who was more afraid at this moment – Bethany, of death; or the beast, of what it meant if it couldn't go through with this particular suppertime.

The beast wrapped one of its tongues around Bethany's sneakers and turned her upside down, high in the air – just like it had done in so many of her nightmares. It flared its fangs, and slowly started lowering her towards its belly.

"Don't do it!" begged Ebenezer. "You're better than this, beast. Anyone can change, any time they choose!"

The beast's mouth was wide enough now to lower Bethany past its rows of teeth without slicing her apart. If Bethany had opened her eyes, she would have caught sight of the beast's long and winding insides – filled with mazes of intestines, bubblingly poisonous stomach acids and treacherous caverns of half-digested meals.

Ebenezer was blinded by tears. He collapsed completely to the floor, letting out one guttural sob after another.

The first sound he heard was the beast belching, which made him sob with renewed frenzy. Then, a second later, he heard a thump land next to him.

"Eurghhhhh!" said Bethany, getting to her feet. She was covered in dribble. Some of the stomach acid had bubbled up and set her jumper on fire, so she was forced to take it off. "That was the grossest thing in the world."

"Oh, Bethany!" said Ebenezer.

He went to pat her lovingly on the head, but then quickly backed away. The smell of the beast's insides was astonishingly bad.

"Oh, *Bethany*," said Ebenezer, holding his nose.

"It's not my fault!" said Bethany.

Behind Bethany, the beast slumped in self-pitying defeat. The gigantic gnomes slowly shrank to their usual size. The Frisbees – now just Frisbees, not axe impersonators – fell one by one beside the unconscious neighbours on the floor. Meanwhile, the hoatzin cage sucked out all the bad odours in the air and replaced them with tinges of lavender and strawberry.

"What have I become?" asked the beast. "I can't even eat a child."

Ebenezer ran over to the beast and squeezed a handful of its blobby flesh.

"What are you doing? Are you attacking me?" asked the beast.

"I'm trying to hug you," said Ebenezer. "Not quite sure how hugs work."

"Well, stop it," said the beast. "I'm already feeling bad enough, without you adding physical torture to the mix."

Ebenezer backed off, happy to be done with the hugging business himself. The beast looked at Bethany with disgust dripping out of its eyeballs.

"I *hate* you," it said.

"Not as much as I hate you," said Bethany.

"Then why couldn't I eat you? One little chompedychomp, and you would have been finished," said the beast. "It's finally happened. I've gone weak and widdly."

"Not weak and widdly," said Ebenezer. "Just something new."

"I don't like it. I don't like it one little bit," said the beast. "And I guess I'll have to live with not liking it for the rest of my life – locked away in some stupid laser cage, with a bunch of D.o.R.R.i.S. agents on the other side of the world."

Ebenezer and Bethany exchanged a glance. Ebenezer wanted to keep the beast, but he knew that Bethany wouldn't like the idea.

"I guess you will," said Ebenezer. "I'll come and visit you, though."

"Nah," said Bethany. She couldn't believe the words that were about to come out of her mouth. "You won't be visiting the beast, 'cause the beast isn't going anywhere. It's coming home with us. I don't trust that it won't try and go back to its old self, if we don't keep an eye on it."

"We can try and help it become good!" said Ebenezer with excitement. "Just like we're trying to help each other be good!"

"I'm going to vomit," said the beast. "And I'm not talking about the magical stuff."

Ebenezer clapped his hands, delighted at the thought of all the do-gooding they would do together – and all the praise that would follow. Although he would have to keep telling himself that the praise wasn't necessarily the most important part.

The beast and the Bethany looked at each other, grudgingly resigned to their fates.

"Put me out of my misery then," spat the beast. "Where do we begin with this 'being a better beast' nonsense?"

Bethany and Ebenezer looked around the devastated sweet shop. It seemed a pretty good place for them to start.

"Could you vomit us out some dustpans and brushes?" asked Ebenezer.

The Feathery Farewell

The beast went a few steps further than dustpans and brushes.

It turned the canoe to glass, and then turned the glass into replacement windows. It got the post box to eat up all the hate mail. With a wiggle of its fingers, it replaced the gnomes' gardening hats and tools with chef hats and cooking equipment – and ordered them to fix all the damage that had been done to Miss Muddle's sweet displays.

Then, when the spider-tidiers had got everything back to some semblance of order, the beast started waking people up by slapping the Frisbees across their faces.

The first person it woke up was Mortimer. Ebenezer

and Bethany had lifted him out of the canoe, but they hadn't untied him. They removed the bandages the beast had vomited out to reveal a pair of freshly grown talons.

"*Beast . . . beast . . .*" the parrot murmured weakly, then more strongly as the life returned to his eyes. "Beast! Beast! I've got to stop the beast!"

The beast gave Mortimer its best shot at a smile. The result was absolutely terrifying.

"Many people have tried to kill me. Lady Morgana, the beast known only as Rapscallicus, the armies of Troy – at one point a particularly vengeful goat named Bernard," said the beast. "But I think you came the closest. I'm curious. Why did you try?"

"I did it for Claudette," said Mortimer. "Everything you did to her –"

"You didn't do it for Claudette. You did it for yourself, out of fear and hatred. Trust me, I know," said Bethany. "Claudette had nothing to do with it."

Mortimer struggled to sit up. He opened his beak.

"Stay absolutely silent or I'll boil you into a soup," said the beast. "I'm a bit new to all this, but I think I might have a better way to make things right with Claudette."

The beast wiggled its fingers to make one of the Frisbees

slap Claudette in the face.

Mortimer hadn't noticed she was in the sweet shop, and welled up when he saw her.

"Claudette!" he cried.

"*M-M-Morty?*" said Claudette.

She tried to stand up, but the beast used the Frisbee to slap her back down.

"Don't be a fool. Any sudden movements, and you'll probably perish. That would be really selfish of you, because I'm trying to show off," said the beast.

"*Bethany?*" said Claudette. "*You're alive . . . did I . . . did I . . .?*"

Bethany ran over to her.

"Yes, you definitely helped save me, Claudette," she said.

"Well, that's not really true," said the beast. "I could have turned you into a smoothie any time I wanted to. You just got lucky that today happened to be the day my life changed forever."

Bethany and Ebenezer flashed the beast a look. The beast rolled its three eyes.

"All right, stay still. This might be a little tricky," said the beast. It wiggled its fingers and sent the bandage that had been used to regrow Mortimer's talons over to

Claudette. The bandages wrapped themselves around her head. "There's been something blocking your recovery, and that something was me. A nasty little trace I left in your body to spite Bethany, because I knew how much you meant to her."

The beast cackled. It received another look, and let out a stinky sigh.

"So in order to remove the trace, I'm going to wipe your body and your mind of everything beastly – going all the way back to the day we first met in the bird shop," said the beast. "By the time the bandages are finished with their business, you won't have any memories from that day onwards."

"Hold on, though. The day you met Claudette was the day me and Ebenezer met her for the first time as well," said Bethany.

"How *fascinating*," said the beast. "Please tell me more useless trivia from your life."

"I think she's asking whether that means all Claudette's memories of us will disappear too?" asked Ebenezer.

"Well, *obviously*," said the beast, pulling a face. "For Claudette to heal, I'm going to need to scrub all the memories from the time that she and I were connected. Are you all stupid or something?"

Bethany and Claudette looked at each other. Even though the beast was trying to be good, it seemed as though its vomit was still coming with a price.

"Heal her!" said Mortimer, as he wriggled against his restraints.

"I'm not sure if I want to be healed if it means forgetting our friendship," Claudette said to Bethany. *"You . . . you're one of the most important people in my life."*

"You're one of the most important people in mine too," said Bethany. She didn't even realise she was crying, until she saw the wet marks dripping on Claudette's feathers.

"You what?!" said the beast. "Are you telling me that I've come up with this genius plan for nothing? I could have killed her ages ago if we were just going to let her die."

Bethany wasn't going to let that happen. Claudette was too good for the world to lose – and besides, the forest needed someone who could help Mortimer channel his anger into something more useful. She took a deep breath.

"Do it," said Bethany. "Heal her before it's too late."

The beast impatiently wiggled its fingers and set the bandages to work – wiping away every memory of every conversation, dance, flying session and giggle that Claudette had ever shared with Bethany. As Bethany held her, she watched as the look on Claudette's face transformed from love to complete bewilderment.

Claudette slipped into unconsciousness. Her patchy chest sprouted new, resplendent feathers, her wings snapped back into place, and her beak was smooth of dents. As soon as the bandages had done their work, they slithered off Claudette's head and disintegrated into dust. A moment later, Claudette woke up – still in Bethany's arms.

"What the . . . Where the . . .?" asked Claudette. The sparkle was back in her eyes, and her once beautiful voice was now enchanting again. She looked up at Bethany. "Who are you?"

Bethany knew that she had done the right thing, but it still felt awful to have one of her only friends look at her as though she was a stranger. She gently put Claudette down, and stood up.

"I remember flying towards the bird shop to sing a farewell song for my cousin Patrick. I suppose I must have got lost." Claudette hopped up to her talons and scratched her head with a wing. Her bewilderment deepened when she saw Mortimer. "Morty, what the blazes are you doing here? And why are you wearing those stupid ropes around your wings?"

She swooped over and used her talons to cut the ropes free. Mortimer immediately spread his wings and dived straight in for a hug.

"You're acting as if you haven't seen me in ages!" said Claudette.

"I haven't," said Mortimer quietly. "Not like this anyway."

Claudette seemed to be enjoying the hug, but quickly disentangled herself, because she never liked being rude when meeting strangers. She looked Ebenezer and the beast up and down.

"Thank you ever so much for bringing Morty to me – I guess you must have found him making mischief somewhere," said Claudette. She looked around at all the sleeping people in the sweet shop. "I say, is it usual in this part of the world for everyone to take naps together?"

"They're just napping to get ready for a party," said Bethany. She was trying to sound all cool and relaxed, but her throat was dry and croaky. "You can stay if you like."

"All Wintlorians LOOOOVE parties – how very kind of you! I'll have to take a quick flap around the neighbourhood to see if Morty and I can find some outfits," said Claudette.

"But before all that – my name's Claudette. What's yours?"

Claudette held out her wing for a handshake. Bethany looked at it for a moment.

She knew she couldn't say anything, in case it undid the good work of the beastly bandages. And anyway, she had no idea how she could possibly put what they had meant to each other into words.

Bethany realised that the easiest thing for everybody would be if they remained strangers to each other.

"Did you hear me, poppet?" asked Claudette, with a friendly smile.

"Yeah, I heard you," said Bethany. She turned away from Claudette and wiped her eyes with the sleeves of her jumper. "But I'm actually quite busy – lots to get ready for this party, you see. Don't take this the wrong way, but I think it might just be best if you . . . bog off."

The Changed Mind

Ever the kind and wonderful parrot, Claudette said she completely understood how annoying it could be when people asked you constant questions while you were trying to organise a party. She flew out of the shop with Mortimer, and promised that they wouldn't return until the party was in full swing.

The impatient beast was just about to wake up the rest of the neighbourhood, when another puddle appeared.

Out popped Mr Nickle. He was followed by Agents Hughie, Louie and Stewie – all of whom had a variety of parrots clinging on to them.

"Where's Claudette?" demanded Mr Nickle. "She stole

a D.o.R.R.i.S. umbrella, and she's really in no fit state to travel."

"She is now. I've cured her," boasted the beast.

The old man squinted at the beast. "There's something different about your voice," he said.

"Is there? Oh dearsies," said the beast. It dialled down the slither in its voice, and doubled down on the humiliating baby talk to disguise the fact that its mind was back. "I'm ever-wever so sorrykins if you don't like my voicey-woicey no moresies."

Mr Nickle grunted, satisfied. He picked up the snapped, high-tech umbrella, and looked around at the sleeping bodies on the floor.

"Strange sort of party," he barked. "Sure everything's OK?"

"Oh yes," said Ebenezer. "This is what all parties are like these days. Would you like to stay?"

"Thanks for the offer, but better not. I was in the middle of tracking the Jackal of Mars, when these Dorrises called me in."

Mr Nickle shook his head crossly at the three Dorrises for wasting his time. Then he fished in his pockets and presented a new button to Ebenezer.

"Thought you'd better have this back as well – in case of any emergencies," said Mr Nickle. "Just keep it out of Bethany's way this time."

"Don't worry, wrinkly-pants. No more calls from me," said Bethany. "I've realised you're right. The beast has actually changed."

Mr Nickle squinted suspiciously at Bethany, Ebenezer and the beast, not quite able to place what was different. The parrots jumped off Agents Hughie, Louie and Stewie. They had all hitched a ride to see Claudette, but the promise of a party made sure that they were all going to stay.

"We'll be fine with the beast," said Ebenezer.

"Yeah, nothing's too big for us two to handle," said Bethany. "We're a team on this."

"Byesie-wyesies, Nickle-Wickle!" said the beast.

Mr Nickle squinted suspiciously again. Then, with a shrug, he opened a puddle portal. and he and three Dorrises disappeared.

"Well, *that* was humiliating," said the beast. It added even more than the usual slither to its voice to make up for all the baby talk. "But I guess not as humiliating as this party is going to be."

The beast held out its sticky, slimy hands. Bethany took

one and Ebenezer the other. The beast got the hoatzin stink-box to leak out a gas that would make the neighbourhood slightly more susceptible to suggestions, while the Frisbees woke everyone up. As the party guests yawned and got to their feet, Bethany, Ebenezer and the beast took a series of deep bows.

"Thank you, thank you!" said Ebenezer. "Oh, you're far too kind!"

"We do hope you enjoyed our little showsies," said the beast. "Gaah – our little SHOW! Not showsies."

"We really liked how involved you all got in our performance," said Bethany.

The three of them bowed again. The neighbours, partly influenced by the susceptibility gas, and partly because they didn't know what else to do, began to clap. Dr Barnacle looked to her arm and saw that it was completely healed. The lizard lady didn't know how, but the scarf around her neck seemed even softer and more soothing than she remembered.

"You could have given me some warning, Bethany!" said Miss Muddle, as everyone began to mill and mingle around the sweet shop again. "You had me terrified!"

"I didn't wanna bother you with it, Muddle. You already

had flipping loads on your plate," said Bethany. "And besides, I thought the surprise party needed some sort of actual surprise."

"Oh, um . . . well, I suppose that's kind of nice of you," said Miss Muddle, twirling her blue hair into a knot. "And I guess that it was a rather impressive spectacle. Sorry for getting cross, Bethany – and thanks for helping."

"No biggie," said Bethany, with a shrug. "You didn't really need help anyway. The sweet shop's looking awesome."

"Do you really think so?" asked Miss Muddle, her eyes lighting up.

"Yeah – deffo," said Bethany. "And I just tried one of the new bombastic bubbletrumpets as well. Totally delish."

Miss Muddle entire face lit up – so much so, that it looked like it was in serious danger of bursting into flames. She ran hurriedly into the Concoction Room, but didn't quite shut the door behind her fast enough to stifle the sound of her joyful sobs.

"You making Miss Muddle cry again?"

Bethany turned around and scowled at Geoffrey. "No, I'm flipping not! I mean . . . yeah, I suppose I am, but, actually, I think you'll find –"

Geoffrey leaned over and gave Bethany a hug.

"Hey! I am not a hugger," said Bethany. She didn't try and get out of the hug, though, because she was surprised to find that she was actually enjoying it. "Well . . . maybe I am a bit of a hugger."

"Oh, ah, terribly sorry," said Geoffrey, stepping back. "It's just that I was thinking about that show you just did – and how lifelike it all was. I genuinely thought that beasty thing was going to eat you, and it's made me realise that I need to stop dithering about the things I want, because you never know what might happen. So . . . I was just wondering, oh, ah, well, about this *DI Tortoise* film . . ."

Geoffrey started to sweat. He mopped his brow.

"Oh, ah – you know what, it doesn't matter," he said.

"It does matter!" said Bethany. "Say what you were gonna say."

Geoffrey sweated even more. He fiddled with the buttons of his too-small suit.

"Say what you were gonna say, or I'm gonna shove worms up your nostrils," said Bethany. She smirked to let him know she was joking.

"Ho-righty. I mean righty-ho. No, no, what I mean is . . . what I mean is . . . well, would you like to come and see the film with me? We could see it together, I mean," said Geoffrey. "You know as a date, or a not-date, thing."

The sweat from Geoffrey's forehead dripped on to the floor. It wasn't a good look, but, for some reason, Bethany found it adorable. She made a mental note to control her voice.

"All right then," she said, adding a shrug for good measure. She saw Geoffrey's face fall, so she quickly added, "I mean, yeah. Yeah, that would be flipping awesome."

Geoffrey's face beamed with delight, and so did Bethany's. The sweat pouring out of Geoffrey was now ridiculous, so he quickly dashed off to the loos, even though Bethany had kinda been hoping to try out that hugging thing again with him.

"OOOOOH, Bethany's got a crush, Bethany's got a cruh-ush," said Ebenezer in a sing-song voice, while he twirled around. "Bethany and Geoffrey sitting in the tree, K-I-S-S-I—"

Bethany tugged Ebenezer down by his cravat, until he was at her eye level.

"Shut up, gitface," she said. "If you dare say anything like that again, I'll unleash a plague of moths in your knitwear lounge. Why the flip are you smiling? Don't think I won't do it!"

Ebenezer was dashed close in tears, in fact. Because Bethany had called him gitface again.

"I'm really glad you haven't been horribly murdered," he said, blinking through the tears.

"Suppose I'm pretty glad you haven't been horribly murdered either," said Bethany.

The beast groaned and rolled its eyes.

"Is this what my life is going to be like now?" it asked. "An endless parade of soppiness and sickery? Can we call Mr Nickle back? I think I preferred the cage."

"Oh, come on," said Ebenezer. He waved his hand at the smiling faces, the giggling children, and the secret pick 'n' mix stealers. "You can't tell me that this isn't better than a cage."

The beast shuddered, unsure whether it was more disgusted by: the soppiness, or the fact that a teeny-tiny mouse-crumb part of itself was actually enjoying all the happiness on display. If the other beasts were alive to see it now, they would be ashamed.

Claudette and Mortimer returned to the sweet shop. They immediately headed for the other parrots, and together they all started filling the sweet shop with Patrick's 'Hurricane Picnic' song. For the first time in his life, Mortimer looked like he was actually enjoying a party.

"Is this horrid gloopiness what happiness feels like, then?" asked the beast, shuddering again. "Does this mean that I am a good beast?"

Bethany and Ebenezer managed to keep a straight face for about three seconds, before they burst into laughter.

"Nah, you're no way close to being a good beast," said Bethany, still laughing. "You've got a long, looong way to go. And this gitface and I are gonna be there to keep our flipping eyes on you – every step of the way. It's gonna drive you out of your mind."

THE END . . . ISH

(By which I mean that if you want a happy ending,
you should bog off now.)

The Bethany File

Three months later, Geoffrey was preparing for his first date-not-a-date type thing with Bethany. He was wearing his best and only suit again – even though it was even smaller on him now, owing to a misunderstanding with the washing machine – and clutching a bouquet of the wiggliest worms that he could find in the orphanage's barren gardens.

"Stop sweating," said Timothy Skittle crossly. "You're going to get watermarks all over my paperwork."

"Oh, ah, sorry," said Geoffrey. He used the worms to wipe his forehead. "It's just, ah, well, I'm not sure how these date-not-a-date things are supposed to work."

"I wasn't asking for your life story," said Timothy. "Stop fretting and start filing."

Geoffrey had spent the day trying to distract himself from his pre-date-not-a-date nerves by being as helpful as possible around the orphanage. He had already vacuumed the loos, reorganised the spatulas, fed the stray rats, alphabetised the toothbrushes and sung Amy Clue and her teddy bear Miss Lillipie a moving lullaby – and now, in desperation, he was helping Timothy with his paperwork.

"I can't believe that the beast refused to vomit me out a file sorter," grumbled Timothy. "Everyone else in the neighbourhood said it was such a friendly creature, but by the time I got to the fifteen-storey house, it was rude, slithery and horrid."

"Oh, ah, it'll be back to being really nice soon. Well, soonish. Bethany and Mr Tweezer are trying to help the beast become something rather brilliant," said Geoffrey.

"Fat lot of good that does me," said Timothy. He let out a self-pitying whimper as he looked at Geoffrey's handiwork. "*Please* be more careful with those papers, Geoffrey – look, you've put half of them in that file the wrong way round! There's no point you being here if I'm going to have to redo all your work."

"No, no – please let me help!" said Geoffrey. He looked up at the clock above Timothy's desk and saw that he had at least another two hours before he was due to meet Bethany – another two hours that he'd spend fretting and sweating, if he didn't have something else to distract him. "I promise I'll do better."

"Fine," said Timothy. He lifted a wobbling pile of files and plopped them in front of Geoffrey. "You can get to work on those. If there are any sheets that Miss Fizzlewick didn't sign, hand them over to me."

For the first ten files or so, the distraction sort of worked. But then Geoffrey's doubts and anxieties started creeping in.

Geoffrey was a boy who spent his life in a perpetual state of nervousness, but this evening he was even more nervous than usual. There seemed to be so very many things that could go wrong. Bethany might call to cancel before the date-not-a-date even began. When they got there, the film could be sold out, or the popcorn could be poisoned, or the cinema ushers might be pompous and cruel. Maybe the film itself would be awful – a total betrayal of everything that the *D.I. Tortoise* comics were about – or, even worse, he and Bethany might have a disagreement about it. And maybe the disagreement would cause their whole friendship to crumble. Not only would Bethany refuse to go on another date-not-a-date thing, but she might even refuse to see him ever –

"You've got worms all over that file!" said Timothy. "I can't file worms, Geoffrey!"

"Oh, ah – sorry, I used the wrong hand," said Geoffrey. He apologised to each of the worms before scooping them back into his bouquet. "Won't happen again, I promise."

Geoffrey moved on to the next file. He was almost certain that, in spite of his promise, his mind would drift back to the date-not-a-date. But the file captured his attention, because it happened to be the one that belonged to Bethany.

Geoffrey felt almost guilty looking through it, like he was rummaging through someone's diary. He was just about to move the file on to Timothy's side when something caught his eye.

Several pictures of the moustachioed man, the moustacheless woman and the scowling baby Bethany came tumbling out. The pictures had been taken all over the world, and showed Bethany living the sort of life that could have only been dreamed of by other babies. It had been a life of unparalleled and relentless luxury, where even baby Bethany's catapult-shaped rattle was made of diamonds and pearls. Baby Bethany looked much the same throughout all of them, but the faces of the moustachioed man and the moustacheless woman differed somehow from the beach photograph that Bethany always carried around with her. It was hard for Geoffrey to put his finger on why.

In spite of his initial guiltiness, Geoffrey was now rather pleased that he had stumbled upon the Bethany file. He thought about taking it with him – and began to wonder whether it might make an even better gift than the bouquet of worms.

He flicked through the opening pages of the file, pausing when he got to the parent section. He steeled himself, preparing to read a tragic fire-filled tale. But after reading and rereading the words before him, his eyes opened wide with disbelief.

Soon the disbelief turned to fear.

"Oh no, Bethany," he murmured. "Oh, Bethany. I am so, so sorry."

"You're meant to sort the files, not talk to them!" said Timothy. "Here, I'll sort that one out, if it's too much for you."

"No!" said Geoffrey. He pretended to drop the file to the floor. While picking it up, he shoved all the parent parts of it down the back of his trousers. "There we go," he said, sitting back up again. "All done."

The clock said that it was time for Geoffrey to go. He bid a hurried farewell to Timothy, rushed out of the office – and wondered what on earth he was going to do with the horrid information now nesting inside his head.

Geoffrey was an expert in thinking about all the ways that something could go wrong. But of all the things that could ruin his and Bethany's date-not-a-date, he could have never predicted that her parents might have something to do with it.

The beast, the Bethany,
and Ebenezer will return in . . .

THE BEAST AND THE BETHANY: CHILD OF THE BEAST

Uncaged in 2023

The Wise Meggitt-Phillips

JACK MEGGITT-PHILLIPS

Jackalicious Maggot-Pips has many battles upon his plate at the moment. He's currently at war with the milkman, the tea-mongers, and the overly-friendly neighbour who keeps wishing him a nice day. In his spare time, Jack enjoys canoeing down staircases while crying about the villainy of the beast.

The Wiser Follath

ISABELLE FOLLATH

Izzy-Wizzy Follathykins is a firm believer that the pen is always mightier than the sword. This is one of the chief reasons for why she's lost so many swordfights with rival children's illustrators. She has no spare time, and if she had any, she'd have better things to do than tell you about it.